Praise for

October, October

'Quite simply one of the most beautiful books
I've ever read'
Kiran Millwood Hargrave

'*October, October* is fierce with a wild love. It draws you
into its heart, shakes you with a fury, wraps you in a
spell of storytelling. I loved every page'
Jackie Morris

'Katya Balen's *October, October* is a very special new
addition to the shelf and deserves classic status'
The Times Children's Book of the Week

'One of the most beautiful children's books I've ever read'
Natasha Farrant

'It's EXQUISITE. Read it. Wild yourself. Open your
heart to it. It's like nothing else I've ever read'
Liz Hyder

'Stunning … If you have a middle-grader, or know one,
or are one … treat yourself'
Daniel Hahn, *Spectator*, Books of the Year

October, October

KATYA BALEN

Illustrated by
ANGELA HARDING

BLOOMSBURY
CHILDREN'S BOOKS
LONDON OXFORD NEW YORK NEW DELHI SYDNEY

BLOOMSBURY CHILDREN'S BOOKS
Bloomsbury Publishing Plc
50 Bedford Square, London WC1B 3DP, UK
29 Earlsfort Terrace, Dublin 2, Ireland

BLOOMSBURY, BLOOMSBURY CHILDREN'S BOOKS and the Diana logo
are trademarks of Bloomsbury Publishing Plc

First published in Great Britain in 2020 by Bloomsbury Publishing Plc
This edition published in Great Britain in 2021 by Bloomsbury Publishing Plc

A catalogue record for this book is available from the British Library

ISBN: PB: 978-1-5266-0193-3; eBook: 978-1-5266-0191-9;
ePDF: 978-1-5266-3710-9

4 6 8 10 9 7 5 3

Typeset by RefineCatch Limited, Bungay, Suffolk
Printed and bound in Great Britain by CPI Group (UK) Ltd, Croydon CR0 4YY

To find out more about our authors and books visit www.bloomsbury.com
and sign up for our newsletters

Ruby Lambert, this one's for you

We find the owl at the very edge of our woods the morning after the storm. Wind-blasted and wings flight-frozen and round eyes glassy. I touch its feathers lightly with my fingertip and I'm surprised because they still feel real even though the owl has slipped away somewhere else and Dad is already digging a hole for it in the rain-soaked earth.

I lift its body and it's huge in my hands but the hollow bones do most of the work for me and I almost think the owl might shake the stiffness from its feathers and fly away. I sometimes see flashes of owls dipping through the trees. I hear them calling softly like they're singing night songs to each other and they're beautiful, and like secrets wrapped up in the darkness. I really don't think this one should go into a hole in the ground. I say that to Dad and he says that it's the *circle of life* and that now the owl will *become part of nature again*. Rotting down to bones and feeding the soil with its flesh and growing the roots of plants from its feathers. I almost want to see it happening. Once I found the skeleton of a fox swirled into a circle of bones and scraps of fur. The sweep of its skull and the harp of its ribs were bone-white and beautiful.

Dad shifts the last of the dirt with his spade and sits down at the base of a tree with a huff of air that smokes around him. I put the bird in the hole and mark the grave with a smooth pebble so I'll always know.

After we've buried the owl we walk all around the woods and clear the worst of the damage from the winds and the rain and a little tongue of lightning that has licked the old oak with the branches that spread out like the tentacles of a giant squid. The damage isn't as bad as it's been before and it feels like the storm has cleaned everything back to being new and fresh. I use my hawk eyes and search the ground in flicks and sweeps and I find treasures in the rain-raked earth just like always. Slivers of pottery and something that could be a Roman coin. Gems of smooth blue-green glass. I slip them into my pocket and they bump against each other and clamour to tell their stories to me, but I'll listen later. Now we scrape and chop and rake and tug until half-cracked branches and split trunks are neatened and the raggedy edges of the woods start to look a little bit better.

I help Dad load the best of the fallen branches on to the trailer so we can chop them for firewood or maybe a bonfire, and then we drive the quad over the muddy paths and back to the house so we can unload it into the woodstore. This is my least favourite job because it makes my muscles ache and no matter how much wood I move from the trailer into the store the pile never seems to get any smaller. But I think about the stories hiding in my pocket and I can already feel the beginnings and the middles and the ends start to stitch themselves together in my brain and my muscles work on their own. I reach again and again until my hands touch air and the trailer is empty. Dad and I climb on to the quad bike so we can drive it round the woods for one final check.

Dad lets me drive, although my legs aren't long enough to flick the gears with my feet so he does that bit while he's sitting behind me. We wind through the woods in a circle back to the owl.

Dad says *hang on slow down a second* but I'm already going so slowly that I just have to stop completely and he climbs off the back of the quad. He pushes back a matted curtain of sedge and stoops down. *Come and see this* he says and I hop down and peer into the dark because maybe he's found more treasures stirred from the soil.

It's an owl. A tiny feathered speck of baby owl.

A white heart shape just starting to print on its face. Wide eyes. A minuscule flick of a beak. Fat fragile chest. Dipped in a quiver of soft puffs from its head to the tips of its folded wings.

I reach out my fingers towards it but Dad catches my hand gently and shakes his head. *We have to leave it. Another owl might come back for it and if we take an owl this little …*

His voice fades off and I want to snatch the unspoken words out of his mouth and throw them into the darkening sky because I don't want to leave this owl hidden in bruised leaves and all alone.

He tells me to pop inside while he puts the quad away so I can get a hot drink and warm up a bit before we go back out and sort some supper.

When I'm inside I put the kettle on the stove and sit in my favourite chair. It's squashy and patched up and it looks like it might be a hundred years old.

The stuffing is starting to fall out of one side again and it puffs out like a storm cloud.

I settle in and look up how long it takes for a buried bird to become nothing but those hollow bones that felt like air in my hands, and all the books say six months. So by March the buried owl will be snow-white in the dark beneath me. I don't think about where the baby will be but I cross my fingers so hard that the bones pop bright in my knuckles and I wish that a parent comes back for it.

I read about owls and how they eat mice and voles and shrews. They eat every last scrap and all the stuff they can't digest is regurgitated back out in a pellet. You can see the skin and bones and fur of everything they've eaten. I read about how the first thing they see that brings them food is the thing they will always think of as their parent, even if that's a hand puppet with a mouse in its paw.

I finish reading and wash my sweaty hair in the kitchen sink. I shake the droplets loose like pearls that burst in the air around me.

We live in the woods and we are wild.

Tonight we howl at the star-dusted sky. We throw our voices and shape them and mix them and mould them like clay. We can stretch our sounds so that they reach the very tops of our tallest trees and down to the secret-filled earth and so that they tangle in the brambles and skim across the pond because this world is ours and we are alone.

Just us.

A pocket of people in a pocket of a world that's small as a marble. We are tiny and we are everything and we are wild.

We live in the woods.

We live in the woods and we are wild.

Our house sits in the woods and it's made from the trees that frame it. They've been chopped and planed and smoothed into a house, and so it's not the same as looking at the twisted reaches of the branches but

7

I like to be inside the woods. It feels like a secret because we are hidden away and forgotten about in the best way, even though people know we're here. We have to go into the village every year or so and buy the food we can't grow or the clothes we can't make, which is nearly all clothes except for socks and even those aren't very good when I try. Dad can turn a ball of wool into a foot shape with a click-clack of needles and half an eye on the stove but I can't manage more than a tangle. We get all the things we need for another year and slip back into the woods while the village forgets us again.

The house was built by Dad before I was born. I wasn't born here though, because at the last minute the woman who is my mother said *no way* and she was whisked off to the hospital and she was pushed down corridors that were white and bright and tree-less and blank and like nothing she remembered. But then she did remember. She remembered all the things like microwaves and internet and heating that happens at the push of a button and not from the roar

8

of a stove that makes your clothes smell smoky and sweet. She remembered, and when she had her baby wrapped in a white blanket that matched the walls and the sheets and the pillows she said to Dad that she *couldn't go back*.

She did, for a bit. But she was floating off into the world that fringes ours, and when I was four she was gone. In my head I think I remember the day she left but the memory is like trying to hold water in my cupped hands and it trickles away before my eyes. There are wisps of a woman holding on to my hand and I feel my whole body being pulled along by the tide of another person running and my legs can't keep up. There's crying and I know that I let out a shriek so loud it pierced the sky and the birds scattered.

I wouldn't let her leave with me. I wouldn't leave the woods.

When I try and remember her now it's like she's been sliced out of the memory and all that's left is a black person-shaped shadow where she should be, or sometimes she's there but then her edges

9

fuzz and curl into smoke and nothing's left. I hate her for leaving the wild and I hate her for leaving us and I hate her for leaving our perfect little pocket of the world.

She writes all the time but I don't ever read the letters. I don't know why Dad even bothers collecting them from the wooden letter box at the very edge of the track that leads out into the whole wide world. She's the only person who ever posts us anything. Once Dad opened one of the letters and laid it out on the kitchen table for me to read, but I scrunched up the paper into a scribbled ball and watched it turn to ash in the fire and the inky words fade into the embers. When I was five she came to the woods and I hid up a tree and didn't come down until it was night, even when Dad climbed up to try to coax me out. She did it again when I was seven and then again when I was nine, and every time I scrambled into the safety of branches. Dad says she's not too far away and I should see her and see where she lives and talk to her and be her daughter again, but I stop scavenging and climb up to the top of a tree whenever he talks about her and he doesn't do it so much now. Everything is far away from here and that's exactly how I want it to stay.

There's a word in German that I read about. German has all these strange and magical words that have a million feelings curled up in the letters, like being happy when someone else is sad or longing to be somewhere where you're not right now. I only get that when we go to the village. My favourite one means *forest solitude,* and it's the feeling of being alone in the woods and being calm and happy and safe, and she didn't want that. She wanted me to go to school and spend my weekends with her far away, but then when would I ever be wild and free and climb trees and scavenge for treasure and tell stories by a fire?

I don't want her.

She's not wild like we are.

We finish howling and we let our breath run milky into the night. We gather twigs and the driest of the leaves and the green blush of moss that sinks into tree stumps and we make a fire. Dad produces potatoes from his pocket and we push them into the flames until they sing. I use a stick to pierce them and pull them from the fire when they're cooked, and they smell so delicious that I want to bite into mine straightaway. I don't do it though, not since the last time and the taste of fire and then the hours of swirling ice in my red-raw mouth. I blow on my potato-on-a-stick and just like always Dad shows me the constellations peeping through the tree canopy, even though I can find them all myself. *Orion the Hunter, three stars for a belt. The bears, Ursa Major and Ursa Minor. Lupus the wolf, diamond teeth.* A wild sky.

We head towards our little house when the fire has died and the air freezes the ends of my hair. When I lift my hand to feel them I find crunches of frost like jagged stars. We tramp past the pond and the surface is already pulling tight with ice and I wonder if Dad will let me skate this year with the brown lace-up skates he had when he was my age. He always says it's too dangerous and that the smooth glass will crack and I'll plunge through to the bottom and get trapped under the ice. I just want to glide across the surface like a girl I read about in one of my books and for it to feel a bit like flying.

The house is cold too. I can see my breath inside as well as outside but there's no point lighting the stove now. Dad piles wood up for tomorrow morning and pokes the grey embers inside the belly of the stove to shake any last warmth free. He puts his hand on my head and I lean into him and I can hear the beat of his heart and I am small and warm and safe. He flips the lights on for a second so I can see my way to my room, even though I could do it in the pitch-black dark. Sometimes I take a candle, even though I know the way and even though we have electricity, because it makes me feel like I'm living in the pages of one of my books about children who lived before light bulbs.

My bedroom is little and the roof slopes towards the floor, but I like how that makes it cosy. I have a bedside shelf with a fox whittled from a piece of wood so light it almost floats in the air and a jar of bright shattered scraps of glass and plastic and metal, and Dad gave them both to me, I think. I have two whole walls of books and I like to put them in colour order so that they make a rainbow of spines. I never get rid of them and I can pull one off at random and remember the story all over again and how it felt the first time I read it and what was happening.

I have a patchwork quilt on my bed made from

triangles of material that used to belong to my old dresses and shirts and jumpers and trousers. The shapes slot together into something new and I love it because it's stories from the past sewn together and curled around me. I like to snuggle up under it at night and look out of my window and see the woods dissolving in the dark and listen to the nightbirds starting their songs. But tonight when I hear them all I can think of is the dead owl and the baby owl. I squeeze my eyes tight shut and the images of the blackening woods turn to dust.

But my heart won't stop bruising my ribs, so I wriggle out of bed and open my treasure chest. It's like something a real pirate would have on their ship but instead of gold coins it has the scraps of stories from the woods. It's made from the woods too. Dad pieced it together and smoothed it and shaped it and wrapped it up for Christmas when I was six. Inside is magic. A jigsaw of pottery pieces that must have belonged to a family of ancient woodspeople who lived wild and cooked only on fires and slept under the stars. There are bright bones from the skeleton of a dragon that used to guard the woods with his fierce fire breath, and the feathers of a bird that could mend burns with its song. Whenever I find a new secret in the earth I put it in my treasure chest and it's like my head is full of other lives.

I take the three objects I scavenged earlier and lay them out on my bed. They rattle with stories. The thin black maybe-coins that are bent and twisted and were the last few pennies of a boy thrown to the wolves for being strange and powerful. He could make potions to cure infected wounds and rib-cracking coughs and sweat-drenching fevers, though the villagers didn't trust him. But with a deep whistle and a flick of his wrists the snarling wolves belonged to him and he rode through the trees on their broad backs and they brought him food and he healed their wounds. The slivers of pottery were from the pots that he used to mix up food from the wild world around him. Scraps of vegetables and bright berry spheres cooked over a hungry fire. The smooth blue-green pieces of glass were his magic stones, the ones that gave him the power to fix and heal things that were broken and wrong. I rub my thumb along their time-softened edges and put them carefully into my treasure chest.

Two days later it is my month because it's October. October is the best month when you live in the woods and maybe when you don't, but I wouldn't know. It's when the trees are starting to shake leaves on to a patchwork floor and the ground is bright as fire. The air is crisp with a whisper of frost and the sky smells like smoke. Everything feels new and exciting.

I was born in October in that clean white hospital far away from here. There's a picture of me as a baby all wrapped up in a rainbow blanket and impossibly tiny. It was taken on an ancient camera from Dad's childhood that spits the picture out straightaway. There's no film left any more, but I don't need photographs to remember stuff.

Dad said he and the woman who is my mother

threw names for me around the room, but they bounced off the walls and hit the floor with a thud because nothing felt quite right. They brought me back to the woods and the fire-bellied stove and the birds and the badgers and the falling leaves and Dad said *October* and that name flew.

So this is my month. And we always begin it the same way.

Even when it's freezing.

I wriggle off my yellow wellies and stick my feet into the pond water to test it. The cool silk of mud slips between my toes. I pull off my clothes quicker than a quick thing until I'm wearing just my under-pants. They're the ones with the elastic fraying in white tendrils like an octopus. I can see shards of ice glinting on the glassy pond surface. For a split second I can't do it. I'm as frozen as the ground and the ice and the grass. I'm trapped in the air and I can't move a muscle. And then a bird shrieks in delight and I see it swoop down to the horizon towards some sort of prey and I look at Dad and in three two one we

　　j

　　　　u

　　　　　　m

　　　　　　　　p.

The water crashes around my ears and the frozen
moment shatters into a thousand tiny splinters. The
pond is so cold that I feel like my bones are burning.
I think my heart might have stopped. Underneath the
surface the world is murky and green and I am
suddenly a mermaid escaping from a seaweed prison
run by sharks and I'm swimming my way to freedom.
I kick my legs in the sharp cold and I am lightning
under the water. I roll and push away from the
grasping weeds that transform into hands wanting to
tug me to the bottom. I tumble and weave and the
sharks are swirling in the water and they're closing in
on me and they're so near that I can feel the heat of
their fish breath on my neck and their teeth are
grazing my skin, but at the very last second I grab on

19

to the tentacle of a passing giant squid and he sweeps me to safety just as my head breaks the surface.

Dad is next to me shaking the water from his hair and gasping. *It's colder than ever* he says and he rubs his shoulders with purple hands. We turn and look at each other and we grin through chattering teeth because this firework explosion of cold and shock is brilliant and I whoop into the October sky.

Dad helps me out of the water and we lie on the edge of the pond and look up at a sky filled with lazy stretching clouds. Every year we wait and see who cracks first, and this year it's Dad and he scurries inside to fetch a thermos and the warm dry clothes we hung on the stove, and we sit and sip tea that plumes its steam like the last breaths of the dragon whose bones are nestled in my treasure chest. I pull on thick socks and a bright blue jumper that must be Dad's because it hangs down past my knees but it's so warm that I don't care one little bit. Dad points out different cloud types to me. The altocumulus and the cirrus and the stratus and the altostratus. I point out different cloud shapes to him, the allosaurus eating a fish and the warrior girl on horseback galloping across the blue abyss to save her home from a flint-eyed smoke-filled dragon. Then I tell him the story of the boy with his magic green-glass stones and I wrap us up in his world.

Dad always listens properly to my stories and I stretch this one out until the magic boy and his wolves cure the village of a deadly plague and they know he is good and kind and they want him to come home. But he still chooses to live in his howling pack deep in the forest. Then shivers lick our muscles and so Dad lights another fire in a circle of stones and in his soft green notebook we make a long list of all the things we have to do to get the woods ready for winter.

And that's how we start every October.

We finish the list after breakfast. It's very very very long.

Trees have to be looked after. You can just let them do their own thing and grow and reach and spread themselves sideways and skywards, but it won't do them much good at all. Sometimes it's like we spend all our time lopping and pruning and chopping and taming the trees from trying to grow into each other and strangle one another with their curling branches. The forest is a battleground and I'm a warrior. The trees might fit together to form the perfect canopy of leaves and skeleton branches reaching towards each other, but I know they are in fierce competition, because too many and they all die.

Too large
too small
too skinny
too tall and
they die.

So every October we coppice. We chop down enough trees to let the others grow and for the stumps to have the chance to start again. We shape the trees and hold them and pin them into their places and help them live all together in a muddle of trunks and wood. Sometimes I feel a hot sick sense of shame at stopping the roar of nature, because we're stepping in and using sharp metal and thick twine to tame the forest's instincts, but if we don't do it then there'll be nothing left. And a tree that has been cut down to the ground again and again and again is a tree that can live forever, and that's something that makes my head buzz.

I'm not allowed the growl of a chainsaw in my hands like Dad has in his. I ask every year and every year he says *October, October, not yet, not yet.* He never says my name once when he can say it twice, like it's the words to a song and the sound rises like music.

I'm allowed a small machete which is sharp enough to slice through branches and bones. I have to wear a special shirt that is hot and itchy and that's supposed to stop the tooth-sharp knife slicing through me like I'm made of butter. I've never slipped though. Not once.

We slice and cut and tie and pin until I can see the sun sneaking into the middle of the sky through the canopy above. My hands are full of splinters that feel like they could grow into trees beneath my finger-nails. Dad's hands are rough and tough and the splinters can't break into his skin any more.

I don't know if it counts as the *circle of life* if we're allowed to do something to stop the trees dying, because we're allowed to change the trees but we're not allowed to pick up the baby owl and it doesn't really make much sense to me.

When I start to feel tired and my muscles are stretched and stringy we walk to the growing tunnel to see what we can pick to cook later. We grow our food here and in the winter that is mostly potatoes. Summer means jewel-bright ruby tomatoes and emerald beans glittering from neat earthy beds with opal cabbages and the topaz shimmer of yellow courgettes. There's not as much colour in here in the winter but there's always something we can make, and if not the freezers are full of the summer colours. The only thing we can't make is cheese – or milk – because Dad doesn't want a goat or a cow, so he swaps vegetables for them with Bill the dairy farmer. Bill is our nearest neighbour but he feels a hundred million miles away and we can only get there if we take the rusty Land Rover up the winding forest track and into the world beyond.

The growing tunnel is hot and humid and I imagine

I'm stepping into a jungle. The empty strawberry plants tied to wooden poles transform into vines and the runner beans slither their way into snakes. The red flash of nasturtiums are the furious eyes of a tiger lurking in the undergrowth. I grip my machete and swing it from side to side, because I was raised by tigers and I'm not afraid. His flower eyes widen in surprise and he bows his head right down to his furry paws. He wants to carry me on his back and parade me around because I'm the Queen of the Jungle. Wilder than the jaguars and alligators and snakes so poisonous they could kill you just by breathing near you. Wilder than the rushing rivers filled with piranhas that can eat a whole human in thirty seconds. We gallop through the heatsticky air and twist down paths lined with serpents and frogs and jaguars and a lion with a mane that if you look very closely is made from cabbage leaves. Monkeys chatter excitedly and an owl hoots, and when I hear that I feel heartsore about the baby owl all over again. The animals' voices start to rise above the noise of the jungle and they sound so familiar because they're saying my name.

I am pulled from the jungle and it swirls away like water racing down a plughole. Dad says *October, October, stop swinging your machete around or you'll take my head off* and then he starts to pick the last of the beans from the snakes that are shrinking back into plants with a hiss.

In the tunnel Dad is passing me vegetables to put in a basket and I nibble the end of a bean.

As the basket grows into a bright mountain of carrots and peppers and beans I tell Dad about the jungle that grew all around us and the animals making me their queen, and I don't mention the owl I heard calling to me.

Afterwards Dad drives off in the Land Rover to see Bill the dairy farmer, and I run back into the wild to stop the hoots of the owl echoing in my ears.

I'm going searching.

Searching is my favourite thing to do in the woods. I have a tiny trowel and I have a bucket and I am a detective. I dig through soil and I hunt through bushes and I scour the earth for its secrets.

My feet take me to the owl stone before I've even realised what they're doing. I am a secret agent carefully sneaking through the undergrowth to surprise a criminal gang who have stolen a pirate's treasure map, which contains all the secrets that will unlock a fortune. I am tiptoeing as quietly as I can on a floor littered with crunchy leaves specially planted by the criminals to alert them to sneaking people. I can hear the soft sounds of their whispered conversation and see their twisted shapes shadowed behind trees. The soft sounds start to get louder and louder and more shriek-like. I shake my head and the criminals dissolve into the dawn, but the noise is still there. It rolls between a hiss and a growl. My heart starts to jump and I wish I had my machete or a tiger. There's a rustling too and it's not the normal scuffle of leaves and branches twitching in the wind.

I remember that I am wild and that these are my

woods and I shout into the lightening air that I am October and that I have a machete and a tiger.

No one responds, which is normal because no one ever has, but my palms are slippery. The growling is softening into something else. I take a few steps towards the rounded pebble that sits above the earthbound owl. The sound gets louder and so does the beat of my heart in my ears.

I sweep back the sedge and see the hook of a beak and a flash of a tiny white cloud. A still-alive baby owl roaring at a world that isn't feeding it.

One owl is dead and this one doesn't have a mother any more and another owl hasn't swooped down to save it.

I know I should leave it.

Dad said it wasn't right for humans to take owls.

But we don't let the trees die.

When I shuffle closer to the squeaking owl it doesn't try to move away from me. It's too little and it's too scared and I don't know how this one isn't dead as

29

well, because it's been out here in the cold all alone. It is very small and very young and its eyes aren't even open yet.

I reach out my fingers again and brush the fluff that will one day be rippled feathers. It's so soft that it feels like I'm touching warm air. *Hey hey hey* I whisper and it turns its tiny head towards the sound of my voice and I feel a tug in my chest. *You're OK* I say and I feel its trembling heart.

I remember a book I read a long time ago when I was just learning to stumble through words like each sound was a scrub of undergrowth to battle through and get to the end. I remember a baby barn owl scared of the dark and not knowing that the night was exciting and kind and fun and necessary and wonderful and beautiful. This owl is all alone and the whole world is frightening and pitch-black dark.

I take off my rainbow scarf and use it to scoop the owl up. It struggles weakly and I wrap it loosely so its wings can't beat in a panic and so its sharp talons are caught in fabric. It feels fragile and breakable and I think of hollow bones and the broken body of its mother, who was much bigger and stronger.

I lift the quivering parcel to my chest and I hum. The vibrations bounce through my ribs and into the owl and it stops moving. My tummy lurches because I think it might be dead all of a sudden, but when I peer through the woollen folds I can see its head swivelling and suspicious.

I carry the baby owl to my den. My den is hidden away so carefully that if you weren't looking for it you wouldn't know it even existed. I think Dad pretends not to know about it, but it took me three days to build last summer and I had so many splinters that my hands didn't work as hands for a week afterwards, so he must realise.

The den is like a tent made from felled ash trees, because they're thin enough for me to move by myself and they're tall enough to make a proper shelter so I'm not crouching all the time or hitting my head on branches. My last den wasn't very good. This one is perfect.

The ground is covered with a waterproof tarpaulin I took from one of the sheds. Over the top I've layered blankets and cushions so that it's cosy. The blankets are all different colours and some of them are unravelling because they're ones Dad made before he was very good at knitting. The woman who is my mother taught him, but I haven't used any of her blankets in here. I used to have one on my bed but I balled it up and shoved it in a wardrobe years ago. It was navy and it had yellow stars stitched on in the shape of an O for October.

There's a lantern and a kettle and a chest, which contains a battered metal flask and a box of teabags and a tiny misshapen saucepan and a chipped camping mug and a box of matches and some firewood and kindling. I've been slipping things into the pockets of my coat when I know they won't be missed. The lantern was abandoned in the corner of one of the sheds, but it's beautiful and when I light it the flame throws out purples and blues and greens from its stained glass and the walls of my den come alive with colour. There are also two tins of baked beans, which are left from the ones we bought in the last big shop in the village. The lights in the supermarket hurt my eyes and the rattle and scrape of the trolleys and the sudden *beep beeps* from nowhere and the voices that boomed from the ceiling hurt my ears. So I went and waited in the Land Rover, and when Dad came out he had all these things that I sort of remembered from when I was younger but like they were from a dream. Baked beans and tinned kidney beans and cans of thick red soup and these little dried pellets called lentils. We've still got some of those left.

I put the owl down on a cushion and loosen the scarf from around its claws. It angles its stuck-shut eyes up at me from its rainbow tangle and it doesn't try to get up. I stroke the beginnings of feathers.

I don't know what to do with you I say.

I look out of the door of the den. The sun is hanging low in the sky and weakly reaching out with a watery winter light. Dad won't be back for a while. A firework of fear tingles to the ends of my fingers because

33

he's going to be cross with me for interfering, and Dad never gets cross.

The owl makes a soft sound and I think about how hungry it must be. *I don't think owls eat baked beans* I say. *I read that you like shrews. I don't think I can find you any shrews right now.*

My stomach drops a bit when I think about finding the owl some food. I see shrews and mice and sometimes voles darkly scuttling on the forest floor, but they move like there's a secret electricity running through their bodies. I could never be fast enough. And even if I could catch one, what would I do next?

I could give you a name I say. I try out a few from my books, and just like the names that Dad tried out when I was born they sink to the floor, and the owl keeps swivelling its head slowly.

Pongo

   Perdita

      Mary

Charlie

Joe

    Jane

Carrie

    Paul

George

Posy

  Petra

    Harry

Diggory

    Sara

Cyril

  Anthea

Zack

  Tom

Anne

  Miranda

Clunk. Clunk. Clunk. Swivel. Swivel. Swivel.

The owl is all alone and living in the cast off rubbish of a wood. Scraps of leaves and clods of earth and fractured twigs. Fragments of a story I've read in a book start to puzzle together in my mind. A boy all alone among the rubble of a dump. No parents or friends or family and not part of the world that roared above the walls of his den. The name jumps into my head as if it was always there from the moment I saw the owl and just waiting to show itself.

Stig.

And the name soars.

The tips of my toes are starting to go numb and prickly even though I'm wearing two pairs of thick socks and my boots. If I'm cold then I think that Stig must be close to freezing without the protection of a nest or the warmth of its mother and father and its brother or sister. This last thought gives me a lump in my throat that I swallow away. I open the chest with a creak and take out the firewood and kindling and matches.

I make a small fire a few feet away from the entrance to the den. I do it just like Dad taught me. A circle of stones. A layer of kindling. A pyramid of wood. I strike a match and touch the dancing flicker to the bottom of the pile and watch it *whoooosh* into sparks and flame.

I open the flask of water. It smells like metal and dust but it'll be all right because I'm going to boil it anyway. I pour it into the tea kettle and when the flames are softer and less angry I push it into the middle of the glowing embers.

I put a teabag in the cup and wait for the kettle to sing. The noise runs straight to the back of my brain and it makes the owl shriek with fright, so I hook the kettle out of the fire quick smart and spill bubbling water on to the leaves and they steam. I dribble the rest of the water into my cup and wish I had some milk.

I sit on a tree stump with the owl on my lap and keep stroking its face and drinking my bitter tea and ruffling the edges of the fire with the stick to keep it burning. *It's going to be OK. It'll be OK.*

And I wait for Dad to see my smoke signals.

When the sun is as high as it can possibly reach in the sky I hear the choking splutter of the Land Rover. The engine coughs and I can smell the petrol clinging to the air. The noise stops and the door clunks and then everything goes quiet. Dad will be hauling the milk and cheese and whatever else Bill has offered into the house. I cradle Stig and hum again because it seems to like that.

I hear the strains of Dad's voice calling through the trees, but the words are whipped away by the wind. I can tell from the distant footsteps that he's following the smell of the smoke, but in a sudden instant I don't want him coming here to my secret den. I wrap the owl with quick movements that make it squawk and try to flap its wings in a beating panic. *Shhh shhh* I whisper into where I think its ear must be as I lift it back up to my chest and snake round the back of a group of cedars that block the den from view.

Dad is on one of the paths and he's sniffing the air. The smoke is being carried in a whirl around him and it's hard to tell where it's coming from. I crunch the leaves behind him and he whips round and gives me a grin. He says *I hope you've been doing some home-work* and then he looks at me again and says *October, October, what's that you're holding?*

I think about pulling a story from the air and spinning it into a shape that tells him I didn't have a choice and how I plucked the owl from underneath the shadow of a looming buzzard with fire in its eyes, and Dad would be lost in the threads and he wouldn't be cross, but instead I keep my mouth buttoned and my story inside.

He's not cross exactly.

But he's not exactly happy.

We've brought Stig into the house and Dad has found a deep box to put her in because that's how barn owls nest and that's what Stig is. I don't like calling her *it* so I decide she's a girl and Dad will look up if she definitely is later. While Dad runs his hands over Stig's tiny quivering body and feels her wings I slip the smooth glowing blue-green healing stones into her box. Stig bites Dad but not that hard, though he yelps anyway and I laugh but quietly because I want him to like Stig. Dad is opening one of his huge nature books on the kitchen table and running his

41

finger along the pages. He looks up and he says *we need to get Stig some mice or some chicks* and my stomach scrunches because I've already thought about this and I don't know how to help. But Dad is standing up and getting the keys to the Land Rover and he says *give your face a quick wash because we'll have to go to the pet shop* and I shriek because you can't feed someone's pet to an owl and because I don't want to leave Stig. But Dad looks at me and he says in a voice that's steady and calm *you picked up that owl and now you have to take responsibility.*

I go and wash my face.

I feel sick in the Land Rover. Stig sits in my lap and she doesn't make a peep, even when we *bump bump bump* up the muddy track, and suddenly the trees are fading and the light is bursting from the sky and there's nothing to hold me in and stop me falling away into the edges of the world.

I close my eyes for the rest of the journey and I don't open them until I hear the old-bones creak of the handbrake and the engine stops roaring, but my ears are filling with other noises that bounce from every direction and they're crushing me.

We don't go to the village much. The smell of petrol and the rattle of the Land Rover's engine starting up make my hands sweaty and my heart tight. Dad doesn't like it either. The roar of noise and the push of people and the bright lights of shops and the sharp shape of houses pushing themselves into a treeless sky. My hand always slips into Dad's and I feel small and crushed by the architecture and stamped down by the wall of sound that spills from every angle and demolished by the scents that whip around me. In the forest I can pick out the sound of a bat chittering and find the exact tree where it has made its home. I can catch the scent of rain on the air and the snow before it falls. In the village my senses squash together until everything that hits them is just a tangled scream.

When we last went to the village for our once-a-year trip a man said to Dad that I was funny in the head because I never saw anyone or played with anyone and I didn't go to school so I couldn't know anything. And I wanted to roar back that I knew how to grow an oak from a tiny green twiggy sapling and how to tame a tree and I knew how to smell snow on the air before it fell and I knew how to be wild. But I didn't say a word and I just felt the blood rush to my cheeks and I wanted to fold myself up like a piece of paper and slip into a crack in the pavement. There were girls watching and they were giggling at me. They pointed at my short hair that Dad cuts with kitchen scissors and the thick woollen jumper that was the exact shade of an oak leaf in June.

Those girls had glitter-spun cardigans and sequinned T-shirts and some of them had the tiny pinprick of stars in their ears and their lips were slicked with something sticky and shiny. I imagined the delicate threads of their spiderweb skirts rustling softly against my skin and then I imagined the lace catching on a tree branch and tearing into feathery rags. They looked at me and talked behind their hands, which were decorated with silvery flashes of rings and bright painted fingernails. I was glad then that I didn't go to school.

Now we're in a car park which has shops that look like giant metal boxes dotted around its outside. They all have bright signs and huge glass windows and there are sounds of crashing metal and shouts and engines and horns and music that thumps faster than my heart. This isn't where we normally drive to and I can't find a thread of anything familiar to calm me down.

Dad opens the door of the Land Rover and the air hits me. It smells like car fumes and dust and rubber and sweat and something thicker that hits the back of my throat. I cough but none of the other people getting out of their cars or pushing trolleys back to great grey metal snakes made of a thousand more or holding the hand of a red-faced toddler or walking fast paced head down is coughing. They're rushing and laughing and shouting and talking as though the smell and the noise and the grey grey grey are normal. I am trying to make the world dissolve around me so I can float in space with the stars pinpricking all around or drift deep at the bottom of an ocean with fish scales shimmering up my legs and gills bubbling on my neck. I put my hand into my pocket and thumb the brass button I keep there so I can slip into its story, but nothing works and I am here.

Stig nestles in my coat as we walk towards the huge pet shop. The strange concrete ground rolls beneath my feet and then I see it. One tree planted in a tiny square of soil bordered by more grey stone. It's a yew and it must be hundreds of years old and from when this car park was forest and now it's alone and I want to cry.

The doors *whoosh* open by themselves and I nearly drop Stig. Dad puts his hand on my shoulder and the weight of it stops me floating off into panic, but I can feel a tremble in his tendons as his fingers grip me.

He looks smaller here and out of place without a background of trees.

We go all the way to the back of the shop because that's what a lady who has a badge with 'Marge' on it says we have to do if we've brought in *wildlife*. The way she says that word makes it sound like it's covered in spikes. We walk past rabbits behind plastic doors and one of them is crouching down and squeaking and a boy laughs at how cute they are and I want to shout that rabbits do that when their hearts are beating a million times a millisecond and that this rabbit is afraid.

A big grey dog on a blue lead turns its head and tries to sniff the owl parcel clutched to my chest, but its owner stops it right away and says *no that's not how we make friends* and gives me a smile, but I want to melt into the floor.

It takes ten thousand years to walk a hundred steps.

We buy boxes of frozen dead mice and frozen dead chicks from a bit of the shop where there are snakes snoozing on hot rocks and curled behind water bowls. I've seen snakes before in the woods but only adders with zigzag skin and zigzag movements, so I never get a proper look. These snakes aren't moving at all and I can see every speckle and band.

The mice and chicks come in thick white boxes that Dad says are made of polystyrene and they squeak when I touch them, and I think for a moment that the mice have come back to life. Dad gets some special tins of dog food, which he says is important for giving Stig her strength back. When we queue to pay Dad takes out handfuls of coins from the pocket of his big coat and I feel the woman behind us stiffen with annoyance. I keep looking down at the boxes and seeing Stig's heartface peering blindly up stops my legs from trembling.

In the car on the way back I keep my eyes tight shut again and I'm glad Stig's aren't open yet and that all she'll ever know is the world in the woods.

At home we have so many books in our house that Dad builds new bookshelves every year from the trees around us. They run across all the walls and stretch from the ceiling to the floor. I like the oak ones the best. Now Dad runs his fingers along the battered leathery spines of all the books that explain our world and he finds the one about Stig.

Dad has already read a thousand books about birds and trees and earth and plants but now he reads pages and pages again and again. He tells me Stig is definitely a girl because the feathers on her chest are already darkening from white and that's because girls have a brown bib and boys don't. He tells me

Stig is hungry and thirsty but she's healthy because she's filling her nest box with some impressive smells and I have to keep changing the wood shavings for fresh ones. He tells me it's likely she'll only eat food if it's moving. He tells me that without me Stig would be dead.

Feeding Stig is horrible. We wrap her in a towel so that just her head pokes out and I sit with her wedged between my knees. I can feel her muscles and sinews and bones pressing against my own and she feels stronger and more powerful than I could ever imagine.

First we have to get some liquid into her because even though Dad says owls don't drink very much he can tell she's dehydrated. He makes a mix of sugar and water and I'm glad we still have a bag of sugar sitting at the back of one of the kitchen cupboards. The crystals are clumped together but I push them apart with the back of a spoon until I can give Dad a perfect smooth powder.

He fills a tiny syringe, which is left over from some medicine I had as a baby, and I hold Stig on my lap.

She is furious as we squirt the mixture into her beak.
Next we use a paintbrush that is finer than eyelashes
and offer her the dog food mushed with water. She
hisses out a howl that makes my skin prickle. I didn't
think an owl could make a noise like that and it
fills the room with its awfulness. I can feel something
like tears hot behind my eyes but I won't let myself
cry, because I never do that ever. *She's going to resist
food* says Dad. *All the books say she won't want to eat
for a bit because she's so scared and she needs to learn
she's safe here with you. October, October, she's safe
with you.*

I feel like I'm killing her and I feel like I'm killing
me. I can't fit the brush through the snapping edges
of her beak and her screams sound like a person
trying to die. My hands are dotted with bright blood
from fierce pecks and Dad whispers *slowly slowly*, but
how can I be slow and quick enough to get the food
into her mouth all at the same time and it's all too
impossible and Stig is going to starve to death even
though I'm meant to have saved her.

Deep breath says Dad and I fill my lungs until they might burst and hiss the air out slowly until my heart stops its panicky birdbeat and we keep pushing the brush into the screaming beak until the mush starts to slip down and Stig's talons curl and cramp in fury.

She eats her mush and she's furious but full and she falls asleep in a huffy hissing ball inside her box. Dad puts something that smells sharp and clean on my pecked hands and it stings my skin, but I don't make a sound because I am wild and brave.

We had to force the food into her mouth for days. It was like torture every time and it made us all shout with fury and frustration and I thought she would starve or choke or die or all three. Dad kept running his hands through his hair and opening books and rereading pages and trying and trying, but nothing worked. Stig's beak was always clamped shut and she started to beep with alarm every time we got close to her because we were being so cruel, and I hated it all.

But then one day when I fling a gently defrosting mouse across the room in frustration it accidentally hits Stig in an arc of pink and white and flesh and ice, and then she is on top of it and it's crunched in her talons and she gulps it down like she's never been offered one before and looks at me for more.

Stig makes strange little hops of progress as the days go on and turn into a week.

Her fluff is dissolving and her scrawny body is plump with the whisper of new flight feathers. She doesn't look like a proper barn owl from the books just yet but her shape is slowly changing. She can't fly yet but when she's out of her box she jumps and skips and flaps like she's trying to work out how to make the ground disappear from beneath her claws. She spends a lot of her time hopping in and out of her box and leaping around the house. The arm of my favourite old chair is leaking even more stuffing and the material is ragged from the swipe of talons, but I don't care.

She gets bigger and fatter and hungrier. She's strong and healthy and I take the stones from her box and think that maybe their story could be true. Stig tears through mice with her beak and her talons and the noise used to make me feel sick but now I can eat my stews and soups with the sounds of bone crunching in my ears.

She produces owl pellets, which is when all the bits of mouse that she can't digest come back up. I use an old rusty pair of tweezers to pull one apart and I scrape away the soft blackness that's threaded with fur. I am gentle and careful because I know that the bones inside could crack. White glistens and I see the snarl of teeth. Tiny pearls in a rectangular skull. A loop of pelvis. Beads of a spine and spears of ribs. All the scaffolding that makes a mouse move and run and sprint and chew.

Stig snatches food from our hands, and every time we open the freezer she will poke her face out of the box and stare at us with eyes that want to pop open to see the world around them.

And then they do.

Her eyes are huge and round in her head and they are the colour of the darkest liquidy night. They are full moons when she's looking at you and they're crescents when she's sleepy or thinking. They drink in everything around her and she holds my gaze. She is beautiful and she's my first real friend and I love her with a fierceness that catches me in my chest.

Three weeks later and it's still my month, even though we're getting close to the end, but tomorrow I am eleven years old. We make spicy vegetable stew with yellow courgettes that have been waiting in the freezer ready for winter. Every summer we pick and package and freeze until we have so much food we could eat a banquet every day for a year. Dad even freezes milk in case it snows and he can't drive to Bill's.

I chop and Dad throws everything into a heavy pan that's older than I am. The courgettes sizzle with the onions and peppers and Stig sticks her head over the edge of her box and hisses. *Not for you* I say, and it's her feeding time anyway so I throw her a mouse. She swivels her round head impossibly far and her beak pierces the white lump as it flies through the air.

Stig doesn't like to leave my side now. She hops after me on twig legs, and even when I use the loo she pokes her face round the door or squawks outside until I come out.

I curl up in an armchair with Stig next to me and do some of my schoolwork, which today Dad says is to draw a map of the woods, and I can't believe he's making me do work on my birthday eve. I lean a notebook on my knees and use a soft pencil that's been sharpened so many times that it's just a stump. I sketch out the tunnel and the house and the clearings we made last year and the pond and each dense dark muddle of trees that I can make my way through blindfolded. The wood takes its grey shape on the paper and I am an explorer scribbling down the secrets of a lost world. I add the secret den and I add the hollow tree stump where I've hidden secret things. I mark the different sheds that dot about the woods and label the woodstore that sits right next to the house. I draw the tracks that circle and loop through the woods and the ones that lead to the very edges of the world. Dad comes over and he traces the lines with his rough finger that makes the paper crackle when he runs it across the smooth page. *You've missed the track to the outside road* he says, but I haven't.

We eat outside even though the cold air makes my lungs ache. I light a fire and I think about being a girl from ancient times and my clothes are made from rabbit skins and the house dissolves into a shelter made from sticks and mud and the fringes of the forest whirl into the edges of an unknown land ready to be explored on the back of my rearing horse. I'll find my way by starlight and I'll discover new species of animals and maybe long-lost treasure buried deep in the curling roots of an ancient oak tree. I eat my hot stew with my fingers and the juices drip down my chin and I am wild.

Dad says *October, October, you were born in October*

and I giggle because he's saying what he says every year and it's like he thinks I don't know. I wipe my mouth with my sleeve and he says *you were the tiniest thing I'd ever seen* and I roll my eyes because there are a hundred thousand million things tinier than a baby right here now. The flecks of ash spitting from the fire and the sharp blades of frosty grass and the black-dot gnats flicking around our heads and the owl peering from the window of the house.

Sometimes I don't like my birthday very much because it always makes Dad talk about the woman who is my mother. Tonight he drinks a glass of whisky and he lets me try a tiny sip and it tastes like smoke and heat and it makes me cough and tears run down my face and the whisky runs down into my belly like a trail of fire. Then Dad's eyes go all soft and he says *you should see her, she misses you* and *she's not so far away*, and it's the same words he says always and they're already skittering around my brain I put my hands over my ears because he's ruining turning eleven.

We stay up late by the fire and when Dad's battered old wristwatch tells us that it's the right time we shout my age at the sky. We dance around the fire and I am back to being the ancient explorer girl dressed in furs and skins. The moonlight dances with us and everything looks ghostly beautiful. Dad looks down at the watch again and whoops *October, October, you're eleven years old and ten seconds eleven seconds twelve seconds thirteen seconds fourteen seconds*, and I wonder if he'll keep doing that until I'm twelve. But then he stops shouting and he stops dancing and he rummages in the deep pocket of his overcoat and he pulls out a package wrapped in crumpled brown paper and tied with the bright orange string we use to lash climbing plants to their bamboo poles in the growing tunnel and he says *happy birthday, little one*.

I ignore the *little* and pick apart the knots in the string. They're tight and my fingers start to ache but I get them apart eventually and the paper falls away like an onion skin. Nestled inside is a black leather glove. Just one. It is soft and strong all at once. Dad is looking at me and he says *it's for you and Stig, because when she learns to fly you don't want those talons getting mixed up with the skin on your hands* and *it's what proper falconers have for their birds.*

I slip the glove on to my hand and it feels like a second skin.

We stay up so late that the sun is already fat and high above the trees by the time we wake up, and Stig is hissing furiously for more mouse. Dad makes me a cup of hot milk in my favourite mug. I sip the milk, which is a little bit too hot. I've just finished a book that talked about hot chocolate with clouds of pillowy whipped cream on top and sticky marshmallows in pink and white. I haven't ever had hot chocolate or whipped cream or marshmallows but today I can almost taste their sugary sweetness.

I get dressed to go outside because we always plant a tree on my birthday. Dad planted an oak when I was first born and now it's taller than I am but still teeny tiny next to all the oaks that are hundreds and hundreds of years old.

This year I want to plant a silver birch, because they shine like moonlight. You're not supposed to plant them until November but we're nearly there and I said *please please please*.

We take Stig out into the sparkling morning and she hops around the ground and topples off her talons because she's trying to fly but she doesn't know how and nothing in her body works quite like it should yet. She shakes her ruffled feathers and bounces off again like she meant to fall and we laugh at her, but gently.

We dig a hole in a spot where sunlight can reach the silver birch because they like that, a spot that's not too close to other trees so it can spread and grow and be free. We dig with spades that crack the hard ground like an earthquake. I am on a desert island digging for long-lost treasure buried deep below our feet, and I'm digging for a secret chest full

65

of mysterious riddles that will lead me all around the world and back again in search of a lost magical necklace made of pearly raindrops that will make me magic too.

When the hole is deep enough we are supposed to spread a layer of compost, which is just rotted-down food and scraps. Dad turns round and looks for the sack he's sure he brought out with him, but it's still in one of the sheds so he stumps off to find it. I gaze into the yawning galaxy of black at my feet.

I kneel down and my eyes search and skim and scan and I see marbled stones hidden in clods of earth veined with plant roots. I find a flattened disc of a bullet and I don't like touching something that's whistled through flesh and bone and exploded into death. There are jigsaws of pottery and rusted

bottle caps with edges like teeth. I run my fingers around the grainy earth and pluck prizes from the soil.

And

then

I scrabble deeper and deeper

and I find

something magical.

I nearly don't see it. It doesn't gleam or shine because
it's so caked in mud and dirt that it could just be
another clump of earth. But I'm the best searcher in
the business and I know there's something there and
I press my hands into the hole and I feel it pressing
into my palm. When I pull it out I brush and scrub
and the middle falls away and I'm left with a perfect
circle.

A ring.

I've never found a ring before. Sometimes I find
what I think were once brooches but they're always

green and twisted, and sometimes there's a flash of quicksilver in the corner of my eye but it's always a wrapper dropped by a thieving bird or the wink of glass smoothed into a pearl. I pour my water over the ring and the gold starts to shine through. I rub it with my fingers but they're as muddy as the ring, so I race back to the house and rinse it under the tap until the sink is black.

It's a thin gold band and it's too big for my fingers and the inside is bumpy and grooved. My heart thumps and bounces because I can't wait to tell its story. It'll be the best one yet and I can secretly shape it and craft it until it's perfect and Dad and I can share it by the fire. It's like the woods have given me a birthday present.

Then Dad comes back and I slip it into my pocket because I'm not ready to share the story just yet. When I do it will be brilliant and it will fill the space around us with another world.

Dad helps me to lift in the silver birch sapling and we fill in the hole. The tree isn't silver yet and it's skinny and trembles in the wind. By the time it's grown to full height it will be nearly as big as a blue whale and it will make me feel very small.

We pack the last of the dark earth around the tree and Dad puts a little marker in the ground that says simply *October 11* so we'll always know. I stroke a leaf and I whistle to hopping Stig and she scrambles over to see and I tell her it's my birthday tree and maybe we'll do one for her next year. I point at the saplings all around us with their little markers. For the first few years Dad planted ash trees because they grow twenty-four inches every year and now they're reaching for the skies. *October 1 October 2 October 3 October 4*. Ashes and ashes. There are hawthorns and elms nearby with *October 5* and 6 and 7 and 8, and 9 and *10* are apple trees. I tell Stig I want an oak next year because they're *mighty*. As I say the word I can feel the weight of the ring hidden in my pocket.

That's when I hear the rumble

in the wind

stones flying and earth crunching

a growl

and a purr.

Dad looks up too and he says *wait here, October,*
October and he strides through the trees and he takes
the spade with him and I am left alone hidden among
the trees with Stig. The sound has stopped and I can't
hear anything but birdsong and the whip of branches
and the sighing of the leaves in the wind but I am
trembling like the silver birch and my feet are growing
roots in the ground.

I don't like this one bit.

L etters

Birthday

Not a surprise exactly

Will she see me

I have to try

I hear them before I see them. I can only hear some
of the words but I know one voice and I don't know
the other, except maybe I do but it's like listening to

something far away underwater. Dad is talking to someone and they're coming this way and in that second I can't remember how to run and there's no den to hide in and I am stuck.

Then they come into sight through the curtain of trees and it's Dad and he's with a woman with dark curly hair that falls to her coat collar which is red and made of something soft and that wouldn't keep out any mud or rain. She's wearing black wellingtons but they're shiny and clean. She's carrying a box wrapped in sparkly paper that reminds me of the tops the girls in the village wear. I clench my hand around the secret ring in my pocket until the edges are bursting the seams of my skin. One of the fingers that holds the box is decorated with a ring that has a cloudy grey-white stone shaped in a circle and the name of what that stone is called whispers into my mind and I don't know where it came from. *Moonstone.*

Looking at her is like staring down a telescope that peers backwards through all the layers of time and memory in your head.

That hair curling damp from the pond water and sharpening with ice.

That ring catching the sun and throwing shapes on the wall.

Me reaching for the ring and that voice telling me it was made of the moon.

That voice bubbling through my skin and into my brain and it zips and *pings* and matches with memories.

The woman with the dark curly hair and the red coat and the black shiny boots and the moonstone ring and the sparkly present is my mother.

She looks at me and she smiles a smile that explodes me and I am four and watching her getting into a silver car and everyone is crying and she's telling me she'll see me soon and everything will be OK, just different but OK. And then the cough of the silver car's engine starting and the quiet rumble of tyres on the track and the feeling of my heart bursting.

I look at the woman who is my mother

And my limbs unstick.

And I run.

My feet beat a path through leaves and mud and twists of undergrowth and I can hear my breath running ragged from my lungs and the shouts of Dad and then the beep of Stig's little voice, but I keep going even though my air is running out. Dad is running too and the ground is vibrating with the weight of his boots and I need to go up up and away.

The bark rubs my hands raw and my skin shrieks. Dad is shouting not to climb and his words catch in the leaves as he follows me. I turn my head to see him and then out of the corner of my eye I see her standing at the bottom of the trunk so I keep going towards the sky. I stretch and curl and reach and bend until I'm higher than I've ever been before and I can stroke the sun with my fingertips and breathe the clouds.

Dad's breathing is getting louder and it creaks in his chest like the branches around us. His words come in little bursts.

October

    October

you're too high

this is too

dangerous
come down can you

get

    down?

Of course I can get down. I'm a lightning-fast jungle girl shimmying up vines and

and

I can't find the rest of the story.

I climb a bit further. Now I'm a mountaineer and I'm searching for an ancient creature that is a half-truth.

Now that story has disappeared too and I'm a thousand feet in the air and down below is danger and up above is the purpling sky.

Dad shouts and moves after me, but I just keep reaching for branches and looping my ankles around the right ones. I don't look down because that's the number-one rule of climbing trees and everyone knows that.

Climb.

Breathe.

Climb.

Climb.

Climb.

And then

a splintering

a creak

a shout

a scream

a crash

a *whoosh*

a thud.

Silence.

And where Dad was there are only broken branches and still-moving air.

And then my own heartbeat roars and I break the number-one rule and I look down.

And he's on the ground in a quiet impossible heap of arms and legs and angles and the woman who is my mother is on her knees and her moonstone hand is pressed flat against her mouth and her other hand is in the pocket of that bright coat that's red like blood and there's real blood too and her fingers are tapping at the rectangular screen of her mobile phone and she's talking and I start to climb down with shaking arms even though she screams at me not to in case more branches break.

He is pale and he's not moving and there's a flash of bright blood on his temple and something darker blooming on to the leaves under his head. I want to shake him awake but she stops me and says *don't move him, October, you can't move him in case it hurts him more* and I want to scream that I've already killed him but I just tremble and put my burning balled hands into my pockets. She is still on the phone but she keeps holding it up to the sky and says *hello hello yes I'm still here yes it's quite hard to find if you just turn left at the yellow sign and then you'll have to keep going even when the track stops being a road oh yes there's a big patch of grass in front of*

79

the house I don't know no smaller than that I think oh but please hurry are you on your way yes yes he's still breathing.

When she says the final bit I let a rush of air *whoosh* from my lungs and I didn't even know I had been holding it inside and I drop to my knees.

In five seconds or five minutes or five years a helicopter churns up the sky and the noise roars and tears the air and it lands on the stretch of lawn in front of the house and orange people skid into view and I am pushed back by arms and noise and questions.

Where did he fall from?

When did this happen?

Has he regained consciousness at all?

Did he stop breathing?

Stand back stand back stand back.

I get up and stand back and she touches my hand. I snatch it back and I stare through the sea of orange shapes but I can't see Dad at all. There have never been so many people in our woods before and I want to take time and rewind it like the plastic tapes that play Dad's favourite music. I imagine the day reeling backwards and everyone drifting towards the helicopter in reverse and Dad flying back up through the air into the tree and then I think I don't want to rewind. I want to wipe it all clean and record it again.

The orange people have machines that *cheep* and *beep* and *ping* and my tummy lurches because I've forgotten Stig and she's back where we planted my birthday tree and is it still my birthday? Time keeps whirling and twisting and I don't know if we've shot through the night and it's a whole other day but I can't remember seeing the moon.

I am stuck and torn and I need to find Stig and I need to stay here with Dad and I need to get away from her. I am rooted to the spot like a tree and stuck fast like the sword in the stone and I can't tear my eyes away from the ground in front of me where a story is unspooling like a nightmare.

When she touches me again the spell is broken and I shatter the stone around my feet and slip into the trees.

I find Stig almost immediately, hiding behind the shiny present that is glowing in the dirt and looking out of place and wrong, just like the woman who is my mother. I think how lucky I am to have found Stig so quickly and then I think how stupid I am because nothing about today is lucky. I pick Stig up and I cuddle her into my jumper and we tremble together as we walk back to the bright jackets.

The woman who is my mother is white with worry and panic and maybe fury and she opens her mouth and I think she'll shout but she says *hello, Stig* and she reaches out a single finger to tickle Stig's softest feather and Stig closes her moon-eyes and doesn't try to bite.

One of the orange people comes over, and if she thinks a shaking girl holding an owl is strange she doesn't show it. *We're putting him in the helicopter now he's stable* she says and *do you have a car so you can meet us at the hospital?* And she and the woman who is my mother start talking about things and I want to shout that it's me and Dad and it isn't anything to do with this person who is so smoothly arranging everything like she's one of us.

On the way to the hospital neither of us says a word or makes a sound, not even Stig.

The hospital is the worst place I have ever been in my whole life. It makes the pet shop and its light and noises and people and smells seem magical and hazy and soft and safe. Here the lights make my eyes burn and stream and the noise is a wall that I can't walk through. The smell blooms in my brain and it catches the memory of my pecked hand and Dad dabbing something stinging into my skin, and it all feels like a different life and this one right now is very wrong. She takes my hand and she pulls me through the words and the screams and the light and she says *we're looking for Ezra Holt, where is he please* and I think that I don't know, how could I know? But then I realise my eyes are

85

closed and when I open them she's talking to someone dressed in blue pyjamas and we're pulled down the whirlpool of another screaming corridor and put into a room with scratchy chairs and posters that say things like CATCH IT BIN IT KILL IT, and I hold Stig even tighter under my jumper.

The blue-pyjama woman leaves and says *someone will be along soon* and then it's just us and a silence that stretches across a million years.

She turns to me and she reaches out her hand and the moonstone flashes the lights back up to the ceiling and I flinch. *I just wanted to see you on your birthday just once I write all the time and you never reply I missed you so much.*

And I snarl like the foxes who skulk around the edges of the woods and I pull away and I didn't know that it was possible to have so much fury beating through my veins and it must be dissolving them and turning my insides black and I say the first words I've said to her in seven years

This is all your fault.

Waiting waiting waiting.

The hum of lights.

The burn of white walls.

The sharp air.

The silence between us.

After for ever and ever a doctor comes and tells us that Dad is *out of surgery* and that there's bleeding and cracks and splits and everything is falling apart. The woman who is my mother is making rushed scribbly notes in a blue notebook with a pen that's leaking ink like blood on to the snowy pages. The doctor keeps talking but her words are too long for me to follow them all the way to the end and I just want to see Dad. I tell the doctor and she looks at me and she sees an owl and her eyes are wider than Stig's and she tells me I can't have an owl in the hospital and that *I certainly can't take an owl* in to see Dad and I start to cry again and this is all so very new because I try not to cry ever and now I can't stop it happening. I want the woods and I want Dad and I want to be held in place by the trees surrounding me. The woman who is my mother says *I'll take Stig for a walk outside, shall I* and I snap that Stig isn't a dog and *you don't know how to look after her, you don't know what's the best for her* and the doctor has left the room.

The woman who is my mother takes off her scarf and wraps it around my neck, and I'm about to shout but then I see she has draped it just so and that you can't see the little Stig bump in my jumper any more.

Dad is beeping. His heartbeat is green lines on a black screen and his breath is numbers. Every breath travels into him through a tube in his mouth and there's someone else's blood dribbling into his veins from a bag and I feel sick and I want to know what happened to his blood but I remember the circle behind his head on the forest floor. It will be soaked into the earth now and into the roots of plants.

A different doctor is checking the tubes and wires and liquids and beeps and numbers and he turns round and he says that Dad will have more surgery soon and so we should be quick, but he says it nicely. I touch Dad's hand and it's cold and stiff and like the owl we found after the storm. There are plastic tubes dipping into his skin and threading through his veins and there are smears of blood where they've bitten him with needles. I look at the numbers and the little leaps of heartbeats on the screen and tell myself that he's not dead he's not dead he's not dead.

The woman who is my mother is talking to this doctor and I don't even try to listen but when she says

October, we have to go now I wish I had tried to catch the words because I suddenly don't know where we're going. I want to stay with Dad. I say it louder and louder and louder and the air starts to become harder and harder for me to breathe in and the walls are moving and getting closer and I'm being squashed and squeezed and crushed and I close my eyes against the lights and the walls and I'm moving through the impossible air even though my feet are frozen and I put my hands over my ears and shout to push back everything and everyone and when I look and listen again I'm in the car and I didn't get to say goodbye.

We drive back to the woods and for a heartleap moment I think I'll see Dad walking out of the house, but then I remember how stupid that is. At least I'll still have my trees and my pond and my birds and my foxes and my plants and my fat armchair and my vegetable tunnel and the wild. It'll be strange having this woman folded into the woods and the house when she's been outside of the lines of my life for ever and ever and I just want Dad to be back home and everything to be the same as before.

I don't talk to her before I go to bed. I load wood into the stove so that it doesn't go out overnight and I make sure there's enough left in the basket for morning. I get some milk out of the little kitchen freezer and some leftover stew so that I won't have to cook tomorrow, and maybe Dad will even be well enough to have some too. I check the batteries to see how much power we have left. It's always harder to catch sunlight in the winter.

She looks at the stove and the woodpile and the generator and the big yellow box that stores the sunpower like a spell in the batteries and she shakes her head and says *I can't do all of this again* and I want to say I can, but I don't because I don't want to talk to this woman who pulled me away from the hospital and who came here and ruined everything.

I take Stig into my bedroom and I shut the door with a crack that makes us both jump and I get into bed under my patchwork quilt and I'm still wearing my clothes that smell like trees and wind and smoke and now the scent of hospital is caught in their seams. I can hear her moving around outside and I put my fingers in my ears so I can pretend she's not here and

I make a tent under my covers and I sit in the dark hot air and I swallow sobs until they burst free and I cry in the dark and I

remember how my screams split the sky when she left.

It's still my birthday.

In the morning when I get up she is already in the kitchen and her face is bruised with tiredness. The kitchen is freezing and my feet curl on the stone floor. She hasn't cleared out the ash properly from the fire and it's smoky and the air is grey and there's a streak of charcoal on her cheek. She is ruffling the scraps of wood and the embers with a poker and her breath is coming in hot bursts and she's doing it all wrong. She jabs the belly of the stove and it roars back and she falls backwards on to the stone floor. There is a moment where the world hangs still and quiet. Then she shouts at the stove and there are tears in her voice and I go back into my room before she sees.

When I am too hungry to stay in my room I take Stig and I thump into the cold kitchen. She smiles but just with her mouth and she makes me a cup of tea and she makes it taste all wrong so I pour it down the sink and make another one and she twists her fingers.

The shiny flat phone buzzes and she picks it up and walks quickly out of the door and to the edge of the woods, where the trees swallow her words and she disappears.

I feed Stig a mouse and I shiver and it's like we're the only two living beings in the whole world.

When she comes back inside she tells me to pack a bag of things and she smiles all brightly like it's an adventure.

I refuse to pack my bag. I refuse to leave. I shut myself in my bedroom and I try to move my bed so that it'll block the door, but it's too heavy and the skin on my hands is rubbed raw. I can hear her outside but I try to turn off my ears and I push my fingers into them and it works for a bit but then it hurts and her words keep floating through the walls. She says please a lot and the sounds are soft, but after quite a long time they start to get sharper. I pull the quilt over my head and fill my lungs with air and then I shout that I'm staying here on my own.

> *How will you look after Stig if you're here*
> *on your own?*

I ignore her because that's a stupid question.

> *How will you look after yourself if you stay*
> *here on your own?*

That's even more stupid than the first question.

> *October, how will you visit your father if you stay*
> *here on your own?*

My breath catches in the hot quilt tent. Questions chase around my brain, snapping at each other's heels like foxes after hares. Could I walk? I don't know the way and it was further than the village in the car. I could drive the Land Rover but my feet don't quite reach the pedals and I don't have any money for petrol and I don't think I'm allowed and what would happen if the police found me and I went to prison and then I could never visit Dad? I don't have a horse or a bike or a plane or even the right map.

I crack open the door and she's there waiting and it feels like she's won.

I pack.

I fill my pockets with secrets.

I am so angry that I can feel it pouring out of my bones and into my blood and out of my skin. The space around me is coloured with my fury.

I get ice packs from the freezer and tip all of Stig's frozen food into a bag and I feel a tiny glint of pleasure when the woman who is my mother quickly looks away from the pinkly melting mice. I fill another bag with books and she doesn't say anything but when I start again with a new bag she puts her hand on my arm and says that we can buy more books in London. I throw jumpers into my bag and pants and all my trousers are ripped and ragged and I hadn't even noticed before. I scrunch everything up and pack the very very worst pair because she can't stop me wearing them and they're mine. I leave the bags on the floor for her and I walk to the car with Stig's box under one arm and my treasure chest under the other. The ring is hidden in my pocket and it is cold and silent and no stories sing out to me.

S he's taking me back to her house. Her house. In London. A city. A hundred thousand million miles away. I looked at its sprawl of lines on a map once. It was flat and grey and angry and tangled. Dad has been to London and he said it made him cough and choke and that instead of sky there are buildings and instead of trees there are buildings and instead of birds there are buildings.

I rest my face against the cool of the window and we drive faster than I've ever gone before because we're on the *motorway* and the zoom of the other cars zipping past makes me grip the seat tighter and tighter and I close my eyes and try not to be sick. My stomach is swooping and it's not just from the zip of the motorway and grumble of the tyres. Every flash of the road that whizzes past the window is another mile and another mile and another mile further and further away from Dad and from the woods and from where I belong. It starts to rain and the drops spatter into larks' feet patterns on the windows until the wind whips them away. I think we'll be in the car forever but there's a crack of the handbrake so much sooner than I was expecting and I forget my silence and I say *why have we stopped* and she looks at me all surprised and says *we're here now, it's not so far, you know*. The little square clock on the dashboard glows the time and I count minutes in my head and we've been driving for one hour and thirty-seven minutes.

Her house is in a sandwich of houses. A sandwich with at least twenty fillings. A long line of the same red brick and the same little windows that peer out on to more house sandwiches and grey pavements scarred with darker grey circles. At first I think she lives in this whole long stretch of building, but when I say that she laughs and says this is a *terraced house* and I roll the words around my tongue. It means the house is attached to other ones on both sides and that some of the walls are shared with other people and you can hear a clunk of feet or a scatter of laughter and it makes me stiffen.

There are six rooms but they are all built in miniature. There are walls everywhere and they divide everything up so neatly that it feels like being on a chessboard. A *living room* with soft grey carpet that makes me feel like I'm walking on sponges or maybe the moon or maybe the seabed. A kitchen with cold squares for a floor and bright lights and white shiny cupboards and a framed painting of a leveret, which is a baby hare. I stare at it and she says *isn't it lovely, a friend of mine did it* and I don't answer because the hare looks frightened and trapped behind glass.

She opens the fridge and asks me if I'm hungry and I shake my head no but I can't stop staring inside. There are so many packets and bottles and tubes and jars and they're all higgledy-piggledy on the shelves and falling over each other and piled up and I've never seen so much food and she must have just done a big shop and then she says *oh I really need to get to the supermarket but there's some yoghurt or cheese or I've probably got some eggs* and I wonder how you can not know if you've got eggs.

The kitchen looks out on to what she calls the garden but there's no grass or trees or vegetable patch or anything but a blank grey stone floor and a little painted table and iron chairs with cold metal swirls swimming up their backs and a looming shed that she says is where she works. It takes up most of the space and its windows blink blankly back at the house. The garden doesn't look like the outside at all. There's nothing alive.

There's a *dining room* which has a metal table and chairs. On the wall is a picture frame but inside it's divided into lots of little boxes and there's no glass on the front. Instead of a picture there are tiny objects nestled in the boxes and I can see a shell and a snap of glass and a sliver of something silver but I stop myself looking because I don't want her to think I'm interested. There's a fireplace in here and I want to light a fire but when I look closely it's not even a real fireplace because there's nowhere for the smoke to go and the inside is pure white and no soot has ever licked that paint. There's no warmth of wood anywhere and I shiver and I want to go home more than anything else in the whole wide world.

Up a skinny staircase there's a bathroom with more cold squares on the walls and on the floor and a bedroom that is boring and white and cold even though there are radiators on the wall that are meant to make it warm. She tells me that they're called *radiators* and I look at her and she must think I don't know what they are even though we have them at home and the fire heats the water for them. It all works perfectly. She takes out the flat phone she used to call the ambulance and shows me that the radiators can be switched on just by pressing a button. *No need to chop wood!* she says, as if she's telling me something wonderful. I love chopping wood and I love the roar of the fire and the heat of the stove's belly and our little house that isn't stuck fast to everyone else's lives.

There's one more bedroom. It has boring white walls and a boring little desk and a boring white bed with a boring white cover and a window that looks on to the grey garden and an empty bookshelf which looks wrong. She says the room is mine now and we can make it just how I like and I think how stupid is that because I'm spending one night here and then we're going straight back to the hospital and then I can take Dad home to the woods and I can do all the difficult things until he's feeling better and then it'll be just like always. I say that I'm not staying and that I'll be home with Dad before you can even blink and she looks at me and she says *oh October, October, Dad is going to be in that hospital for a lot longer than that, my darling* and with a spitting fury that burns like nettles I think how dare she call me that the way he does and I want to catch the *darling* and throw it back at her.

I try to feed Stig in the kitchen, but she turns her face away and closes her eyes. I remember those horrible days trying to push paste into her clamped beak and another little burst of worry fizzles under my skin. I don't say a word to the woman who is my mother as I march upstairs with Stig clutched to my chest and settle her in her box at the end of my bed.

I brush my teeth before bed in the cold white bathroom. The bath is all angles and sharp lines and I miss our fat-bellied tub with its feet that curl at the floor. I miss everything and it feels like acid swimming in my blood. When the woman who is my mother saw my toothbrush she tried to give me a new one right from a fresh packet that she had under the sink, even though she didn't know I was coming. I shook my head no way and she put it in the cup on the edge of the sink anyway. I don't put my brush next to it when I've finished because I'm not staying, and then I spit white foam into the sparkling sink and I don't rinse it away. I don't say a word to the woman who is my mother.

I get into bed. I can see the sky through the window but it's nothing but black black black and not a single pinprick star peeps through the clouds and so I can't find north and I can't tell the stories of the stars.

At home it is not quiet at night because you can

hear the wind and rain and the birds and the ghostly screams of foxes and deer and the shouts of rabbits. But here the noise is different. It thrums through the house and I can feel it rattling my bones. Cars and horns and shouts and laughter and a dog barking over and over and over and more shouts and the low murmur of voices through the walls and the sounds bounce off the houses and the glass and the concrete and fill every inch of space.

She comes in. I turn over and face the wall but I feel her sit down on the bed anyway and I curl myself up into a tiny ball and pretend that I'm shrinking down smaller than a cat and then a mouse and then a ladybird and then an ant and then a flea and she can't see me. She strokes the lump that's me like I really am a cat and I nearly hiss. She sighs and she says *I know this is the worst few days in the whole history of worst days and I'm so sorry, October, I'm so sorry. I've missed you so much that sometimes I thought I would burst into a thousand pieces with the feeling and this is never how I wanted it to be and your dad lived in*

London for a bit before you were born did you know and he just couldn't cope and the woods brought him back to life but it was killing me and ... and then she shifts and in a voice that sounds like it's pushing past tears she says *I'm so happy that I get to see you.*

She gets up and I can tell she's looking at the lump that is me and when I hear her footsteps turning I forget my silence and I pull back the covers from my head and I whisper

I hate you

and every sound is spiky and the words cut the air and I know from the way her back stiffens in the darkening doorway that she's heard me.

I watch the glowing clock on the wall and I see the minutes of the first day of being eleven tick away. I am a year and a day older and I am so full of fury and the whole world is different and there are no night-birds or sneaking out to sit in the trees. I slip the ring on to my finger and it's too big and it rattles around my knuckle. I try to think of a story so I can tell Dad, but the words don't slot together and nothing happens. Instead I pull out a jumper from my bag and I bury my nose into its sweet smoke smell and try to pretend I'm somewhere different.

I try to feed Stig again in the morning but her beak stays shut. I know you're meant to weigh birds to know how much they need to eat and Dad and I weren't doing that so maybe she's just fat and full but I tickle her feathers with my fingers and she doesn't feel too fat or too full. I loop her into my scarf again and we do the big long drive that isn't actually so very far. The woman who is my mother doesn't say anything about what I said last night but I can feel the words burn between us.

When we get to the hospital Dad is still and pale and it's not him because Dad is a giant and this man is tiny. His heartbeat still traces lines on the black screen and the bags of blood and clear liquid still drip drip drip into him. I put my hand on his chest to feel that his heart is really still beating inside him and not just on a screen and I feel the kick under my palm but it doesn't make me feel safe like it usually does. I whisper *wake up please wake up and we can go home* and my tears make the blankets sparkle. I've brought the magic glass healing stones from my pocket and I slip them under his pillow but they don't rattle with their story any more and his eyes don't open and I feel stupid for even trying. None of that is real.

The doctor tells me that this is how he'll be *for a while*. Medicines to keep him sleepy. *Give him a chance to heal before he wakes up.* His insides are jigsawed together now and there are pins in his pelvis and he needs a bolt in his arm and his spine is screwed together. That's the bit they're worried about, and my head spins. I sit back in my chair with a thump and there's a screech and a thunder of wings and a scream and an *oh my God it's an owl* and there's a mess on the floor and on my trousers and Stig is flapping furiously. I wrap her up again but it's too late and her talons have cut my hands in two ragged lines that are pinpricked with blood.

We have to leave the ward. One of the nurses wraps my hand up in a big white bandage that I think will never stay clean in the woods, until I remember with a lurch. Stig is Officially Banned and one of the doctors got a bit shouty about *wildlife in a hospital* until the bandage nurse told him to shut up.

We go to the cafe in the hospital and it's full of people with crumpled faces and sleepless eyes and hands that fiddle and twitch and worry at the paper napkins. The woman who is my mother buys me a drink and I sit at the plastic table with Stig hidden underneath on my knee and I stare out across a grey car park under a grey sky and I don't look at her and I don't touch the cup even though my mouth is full of sawdust. I run my fingers around the ring in my pocket and I think of the secret it holds and I think of scavenging in my woods and I think of the lacy patterns the trees would make on my walls at night and I think of the echo of my shouts in the sky and how I could never imagine anything more perfect.

In the car she doesn't start driving straightaway and she doesn't look at me either. She keeps taking deep breaths like she wants to say something but the words are stuck. She coughs and that must unstick the sentences because they fly out so quickly I can barely catch them.

Not fair

not the right environment

make her ill

wild animal

can't look after her

happier

happier

happier.

She's taking Stig away from me.

On the drive there she says it wouldn't work and she's so sorry and that this is kinder and better for Stig and that she's a wild animal and she can't thrive in London and it hurts more than anything but that we have to do the right thing.

I burn and scream and stamp and shout and I know why she told me when I was already in the car and I still try to claw the door open until my nails are ragged and raw just like my voice but I can't unlock the handle and I throw myself at the window and scream and she stares ahead with bright eyes.

* * *

We take Stig to an owl rescue centre and I howl like the wild thing I am. My tears stain her feathers dark and she looks at me with her globe eyes and her heart face and the man there says *it's best she's here we know what's best for owls and you saved her you really did and now you're doing what's right* and I don't look at him and I can't look at Stig any more because she's peeping her voice for me and I break in two.

They say that I can visit and that they'll do their best for her, but her best is with me. A man called Jeff, who has a beard and not as many fingers as he should, shows me the big wire-roofed sheds where they keep their owls and he shows me the heaters and the cosy boxes full of straw and the toys baby owls like to play with and he tells me there's always a vet on call and he tells me that if Stig's well enough soon she can be released to the wild just like she should be because she's wild and *that's better than a bedroom in London, isn't it?*

I'm wild too and my sobs are wild and my mind is wild and my last piece of my own wild world is being torn away and I'm not a wild girl any more because I am a hundred million shattered wild pieces.

On the drive back to her house I don't say a word.

When we get inside the house I don't say a word.

When she asks me if I'd like pasta for supper I don't say a word.

When she tells me she's sorry I don't say a word.

And when she goes into the living room to sit on the sofa I very carefully take down the picture of the bouncing leveret trapped behind glass and I smash it into pieces and it's a broken wild thing just like me.

I go to bed and the first thing I see is the soft black leather glove that belonged to me and belonged to Stig and I sniff its spicy scent and put it under my pillow. I look through my box of treasures but I don't try to tell their stories and all the objects stay still and silent. Buttons and pottery and bullets and clay pipes and brooches and bones and shiny scraps that must be something. And then the gold circle. The ring. My last treasure from the woods. The one thing without a story because I was waiting for the perfect one to tell Dad and now I can't and I have no stories left to tell. I thread it through my fingers and try it on but it's too big so I slip it into the pocket of my pyjamas, which are a bit too small but they still smell like home. She left a new pair on my bed and they're decorated with tiny foxes and badgers, but she bought them so I put them neatly folded on to my desk.

We go back to the hospital the day after. And the day after that. And for days and days and days and days and days. Every single one is the same. Dad is still and cold and I only know he's alive because of the heartbeating lines and breathing numbers on the flashing screen above his bed. Doctors and nurses melt in and out and time is split into the regular beeps and hisses of the machines. I sit with him until she says we have to go and then she has a drink and she always buys me one and I always ignore it and then we drive back in the dark and in silence.

*　*　*

I sit in the room that's not mine but she says is mine and I think about Stig and I wonder if she'll ever fly or whether being all on her own is weighing her wings down. I read the same books over and over again but I can't make my mind work properly and I can't make the stories come alive so I stay stuck stuck stuck inside these four white walls. I am wild and I am trapped in a cage and my heart aches and I hate the woman who is my mother more than any of the words in any of my books could ever say. I can feel my insides turning black with the fury.

Dad is still asleep. I know he'll wake up soon like in those fairy stories that I always hated because it was always a girl waiting to be rescued, but now I want to believe in them more than anything. He won't have a pumpkin or a spinning wheel or seven dwarves but he'll have me and we'll be wild in the woods again forever. But each day inches past in the same old pattern round and round and his eyes are closed and there's no magic spell and I'm too old for fairytales.

She tells me we're going somewhere special. An adventure. Somewhere magical and full of treasure. This makes me turn my head and I reach for the ring in my pocket that's a secret because she might take that too and it's mine and it'll never be anyone else's. She says that staying inside in my bedroom isn't good for me and I must be going mad and she's right because my muscles are screaming to be stretched by climbing a tree and running in airgasp bursts through the woods and tumbling into the glittery pond and being free. I'm growing smaller and smaller here and everything inside me is dull.

But where we go isn't wild and it isn't free and it

isn't magical and there's no treasure at all. We walk to a *tube station* and she tells me that underneath London is a whole dark world of trains and tunnels and the bones of the long dead and hidden caves and emergency bunkers and secret rivers. I think of all the secret stories beneath my feet and I almost want to dive down through the pavement and find them but I know my stories are buried too deep inside me now too and it won't work.

We go underground and the noise of the trains hurtling like metal snakes through their tunnels and the black of the tracks and the push and squash of the passengers is too much and my lungs stop working. We are zooming through black nothingness and I claw at the air and curl into a ball on the dirty floor and I know everyone is looking at me and I don't care. The train zooms and rocks and screeches and slows and my tummy rolls. There are too many people and too many noises and too many smells and we're too far away from the sky. I can feel her trying to pick me up and she carries me to the door and my feet scrape the ground because I'm too big for this. The doors open with a *whoosh* of hot air and I burst through just in time to be sick on the platform. Afterwards she tries to pull me close to her and I push and fight and scratch two perfect lines down her cheek and try to find some oxygen as we burst through the black and into the sunshine above ground and she whispers that she's sorry.

We get a taxi home and the adventure is over.

And then the world turns blacker than the tunnels below.

She's sending me to school.

No more trips every day to the hospital and no more lying on my bed remembering the woods and reading the same books over and over and over again.

School. The schools in my books have putrid food and ringing bells and stampedes of children and shouting teachers and detentions and writing lines and canes that whip the air and having to ask to go to the loo and maybe not even being allowed and being told when to eat and when to sit down and when to stand up and being made to be inside except in little lumps of time measured in minutes that are the same every day.

She tells me that I need *an education* and otherwise she'll get in trouble because it's the law that children need to learn and that she needs to go back to work and then I scream and scream and scream because she wanted me back here and she made me come to this tiny sandwiched house in this suffocating city and now she's sending me away. She tells me I need to *calm down* and those words hit me like a flame and I am a firework of fury and I explode in a shatter of mugs and plates and cups and glasses and she tries to put her hands out and stop the spray of china and glass but I won't stop until my hands can't find anything else to throw and the sugar bowl spins on the tiled kitchen floor and all that's left is the sound of my breathing.

She doesn't even shout.

The school is so loud that I put my hands over my ears before we've even walked through the black gates. I've never seen so many children, except from here they all look like they could be the same child repeated over and over and over again in grey trousers and blue jumpers and black shoes and the same sounds coming from their mouths. All screeches and shouts and whoops and screams.

I miss Stig and Dad so much. I miss the weight of her as she sits in the scarf around my neck and the feel of her feathers under my fingertips. If we were home she could rush through the woods and beat her wings in the woodsmoked air. If we were home I could

126

jump in the pond to chase away the feelings that are wrapping themselves around my heart. I run my fingers instead along the ribbed edges of my strange blue jumper that chokes at my neck and pins my arms. I'm not allowed to wear my big knitted jumpers and threadbare raggedy jeans because there's a *uniform* and we dress the same, which is the maddest idea I've ever heard. My shoes pinch my toes and the skin on my heels is already rubbing away in small red circles, even though the walk from the house to the school was only five minutes.

A tall woman with a navy coat and a bright red mouth comes towards us and she reaches out a hand and she says *hello I'm Ms Everett the head teacher and you must be October what an unusual name isn't it lovely to have you here* and her hand is still in front of me and I look at it and up into her face which is smiling redly but the smile is starting to twitch and slip a bit. *Shake hands* whispers the woman who is my mother and I don't know how to do that or really what it is so I take the bony hand in both of mine and shake it from side to side the way a fox shakes its prey and Ms Everett's smile falls off her face.

She puts it back on very quickly, but I know I haven't done the right thing and I'm glad. My hands are shaking all by themselves now and I ball them and try to put them in my grey trouser pockets but my fists meet seams because I've forgotten that they're not real pockets at all and how stupid is that? I had to put the secret ring in my shoe which might be why I have a blister but I couldn't leave it in the house with her and I wanted it near me because it's the final little bit of home. Ms Everett is saying *so you've never been to school before* like I don't know that and I don't say anything back because she already knows everything. *I hear you're very clever* she tries again but I don't need to answer that either because how would she know how could anyone know except Dad and he's far away. *Perhaps you'd like to meet your new friends* and I look up again because I don't have any old friends and I definitely don't want any new friends and she's leading us over to a group of chattering blue jumpers and they're looking at me like I'm the fox's prey and my legs suddenly aren't connected to my brain any more and they're trembling more than my unpocketed hands. *Here you go* she says and she turns to the woman who is my mother and says *always best just to let them settle in right away isn't it*. The woman who is my mother tries to give me a hug and I step back neatly and so she turns it into a funny wave and then they both walk off across the gritty playground and leave me to be hunted.

They circle me. They are sharks who smell my blood as it pounds against my skin. They get closer and closer and open their mouths to show me a thousand rows of jagged teeth that will tear me from my bones like ripping paper and they will make my flesh into mince. Their voices bubble around me and there are questions and hisses and shouts and so much noise that it's a wall all around me and I can't swim away because they're everywhere and there's nowhere to hide and I am about to try to burst through the crowd and through the voices and through the noise.

129

And

I

run.

I run so fast that my muscles scream and my skin stings from the wind and my lungs roar. I don't look where I'm going but just away away away from the noise and the questions and the people.

I run until the ground runs out.

There are fences everywhere and I am caged and trapped and terrified. My heart beats like a humming-bird against my ribs. There are shouts and maybe something that sounds like my name but I don't listen.

There is a tree.

I put my hands on the trunk and for a moment the world is quiet. It's an apple tree and it's very old and very beautiful and I start to scrabble my feet into the grooves of its bark before I know what I'm doing and it feels a little like being in my forest. I am about to push myself up with my arms and monkey my way to the very top so I can touch the sky and lift myself away from everything below but I remember

what happened last time.

It comes in a rush. The shout and the suddenly empty air and the heartstop silence and the thud.

Dad fell because I wasn't brave and I wasn't wild. He fell because I'm a coward and because I ran away and because I hid and I'm the reason he's in pieces a million miles away and I'm the reason Stig is alone in a rescue centre rather than wild with me in the woods and I'm the reason for every single miserable moment that has whirled and stretched around me since my birthday.

I unloop my hands and slide gently to the bottom of the trunk in a heap. When a teacher comes and puts his hand on my shoulder and steers me like I'm a bicycle I let him. When he leads me inside the school and inside a classroom and sits me at a desk I let him.

It's all my fault.

I don't move all day.

Bells ring and clang and people laugh and shout and play and work and fade away. I put my hands over my ears and squeeze my eyes shut and I'm being buried underground in the tunnels under London and there's just the cold and the dark and the feeling of being crushed by the world and I scream inside my head.

I don't move for lunch and I don't move for break-time which is when everyone goes back outside and has a biscuit and I don't move even when I'm bursting for a wee. I don't move when Mr Bennett the teacher bends down to talk to me and I don't move when he puts a worksheet on my desk. It's like the weight of what I've done is pinning me to my chair and the guilt hangs heavily in a cloud and I'm surprised no one else can see the fog around me. I sit and I stare at the front of the room until the clock creeps round to 3 p.m. and then I stand up and leave.

I do the same every day for four days. The woman who is my mother tries to talk to me and the teachers at school try to talk to me and the other children try to talk to me and some of them say things that prick and tear at the bubble around me.

Mute

Weirdo   *Freak*

Dead dad

Savage

Stupid

But one of the teachers must have said something important to them because after three days no one talks to me at all. And I sit with one thought bubbling in my brain and it swells and grows until nothing else will fit. *He won't want me back when he wakes up.*

On the fifth day I go to school and it's different.

I sit in my chair like always and I look at the round face of the clock and watch its hands sweeping the minutes away before I can go home. They are whizzing faster than usual when I want them to trudge slower and slower. I know time is playing tricks on me just because I'm willing it to stop because tonight I have to go and see Dad. I've said I'm too tired and too sleepy and too ill every evening this week but now the woman who is my mother has said we absolutely have to go today and I can sleep in the car and have a paracetamol for any headaches that might seep from my brain and *that's that*.

The minute hand swirls once around the circle. Children come and sit down at their desks. Twice around the circle. Chatter and giggles and shouts.

Three times. The list of names and *here sir*. The emptiness after my name. Four times.

October

   October

      October

         October

October

My name again. Not in a list this time. Louder. On its own. And again.

October

Mr Bennett is standing over me again, but he doesn't have a sheet of paper or an exercise book or a handful of pens like before. He gives me a smile and then he says *off you go then* and I've missed a bit because of staring at the clock. *To the library, off you pop with Yusuf.*

I don't know what's going on and the boy who sits next to me with the skinny knees and a red football that he keeps under the desk is standing up and stretching and saying *race you* but that's not fair because I don't know what's going on and I unstick myself from my seat with a roar in my bones and a panic that shivers me and I follow the boy called Yusuf.

There are children swarming outside the classroom. Blue and grey wasps buzzing.

Bits of a white tunnel but not underground.

Sunlight.

The smell of something like rubber and sweat.

Faces too close to mine

Hands

And then

Books.

Rainbow spines and that paper and ink smell. I sit down with a thump on a lumpy round cushion that sinks wherever I touch it and rattles when I move and the walls are made of books.

It's a bit like home.

The boy called Yusuf is pulling books off the shelves until they bounce and puddle at his feet and I can feel them getting bruised and battered and I feel the words growing inside me until they're big enough to rage out of my mouth and I shout *stop it you're hurting them* and he turns round and looks at me as if I'm a lunatic.

And then he grins at me and he picks up a book and strokes it gently with his thumb like it's an animal and he says *I bloody knew you could talk human.*

Yusuf and the other children in my class think I was raised by wolves. Just like in *The Jungle Book*.

I quite like this.

Yusuf and I are here to research a project. It can be on anything we choose as long as it's history, which as Yusuf says could be *anything from a second ago couldn't it* so why don't we just do what he had for breakfast (Coco Pops, which sound disgusting) and then have a sleep in the corner of the library on the *beanbags*, which are the lumpy cushions I sat on when I first came in.

I don't think what he's saying sounds right, but he's been at school *for years* and I'm brand new so I sit down next to him and he tells me that every class has two people that do special projects together. When the project is finished there's a big showing of them at an *assembly* and sometimes they invite parents if it's really good, which makes my tummy go wriggly because the word *parents* is sticky and difficult. Flickers of guilt and shame lick at my insides and gnaw at my bones.

Dad won't want to come. Not after what I've done to him.

It's always the naughty ones they make do it Yusuf continues because he hasn't noticed the guilt fog that's swirling from my skin again and he flicks a loose bean that's really a funny tiny light white ball at the ceiling. *You're not naughty but you are weird and you don't talk and it's not because you only speak wolf.*

Howling at the sky with Dad. I swallow the memory and I look up at the yellow orb on the ceiling that is throwing out a sickly light that's nothing like real light and I lift my chin and I

H O W L.

And the howl is rage and fear and fury and sadness and something else that is new and twists at the edges of my feelings and it might be excitement and the sound stretches up and reaches to the very corners of the ceiling and it doubles because

Yusuf is howling too.

And we howl at the library moon until a cross face pokes itself round the door and tells us to *get on with your work* and then we laugh instead and then the hot black guilt *whooshes* back into my brain.

We lie back on the beanbags and Yusuf kicks off his black shoes, so I do the same and there's a *ping* and Yusuf says *what is that?*

S o I show him. He lifts the ring up to the light and he twirls it on his thin fingers and he holds it up to his eye. *Wonder what the secret is* he says and tilts it towards the sunlight. *Do you know?* And I don't know what he's talking about at all except that the ring is my secret but how could he know that? *The writing, dummy. You can read can't you? Or did the wolves not teach you?* I open my mouth to remind him that there aren't any wolves in my wood or any wood in England but he doesn't give me the space to speak. He shoves the ring nearly into my eye socket and points. *There.*

On the inside are letters so tiny that you can only see them when the sun and shadows are just right.

Let friend nor foe this secret know.

A secret. A secret hidden in the curve of a ring that was hidden in the heart of my wood. I can feel a little spark of something start to fizz inside me for the first time since the crack and the suddenly empty sky and the whistle of Dad falling. I'll find the secret story for him. I'll tell him and it'll be perfect and it'll be better than anything else and it'll pull him back to those nights by the fire with story-sharing and potatoes and hot tea and maybe he won't hate me. Maybe he won't want to leave me here in London with her.

Yusuf is saying *what if it's a curse* and *what if it leads us to a pirate's hoard* and *what if we get a thousand wishes no a hundred thousand no a million no infinity wishes* and his eyes are shining. He wants to know the secret maybe even more than I do and I didn't think that could ever ever be possible. It's like he grew with the magic of it all and he is stretched with the secret and he fills the space around us with his questions.

The bell rings and I put my hands over my ears and Yusuf rolls his eyes and says that our howls were way louder than the stupid bell. He picks up the books he'd dropped and shoves them back on the shelves and I straighten their crooked spines and stand them up tall. *Come on it's breaktime* he says and shoots out of the door and into the beehive corridor.

So I follow him to the grey playground with its circling sharks and the wall of sound nearly knocks me over. Yusuf shouts *October* across the noise and I follow the sound and find him holding out his red shiny ball. He grins and shows me every single one of his teeth and says *can you play football?*

It turns out I can't play football and it turns out that the grey gritty ground can take the skin off your knees just like sharks' teeth but I don't care even when the blood soaks through my new trousers. When a whistle blows and it's time for the lesson bit of school I have listened to a hundred million questions all about me because Yusuf has told them I can speak both wolf and human. When he tells them I'm a wild girl from the wild woods they all say it's *cool* and a girl asks *do you just get to stay in bed all day if there's no school* and my brain fizzes with all the wonderful ways I used to spend my days. The climbing and the planting and the chopping and the windwhip on my cheeks when I was driving the quad harum-scarum through the leaves and the sharp shivers of the pond water and the lull of the birdsong and how empty my days are now even though everything around me feels so huge and the woods are so far away that tears almost pinch. I can't say anything and I look at Yusuf because he has a million words always ready on the tip of his tongue and he grins and says *October is a treasure hunter.*

Back in the classroom Mr Bennett looks up from his desk and he says *October, Yusuf, what did you decide for your project* and my mouth is wood shavings but Yusuf says quick as a flash *oh we're researching the breakfast habits of people from different centuries, sir* and Mr Bennett raises his eyebrows ever ever so slightly but he nods and says *well done, good work team.*

Now that I'm unfrozen and paying a bit of atten-tion and not watching the circle of the clock school feels very different. The lessons are too quick and too slow all at once. Worksheets are handed out and pencils are sharpened and Mr Bennett writes things on a white screen at the front of the class and some people make stupid noises but Yusuf and another girl throw their pencil shavings at them and they shut up because people seem to think whatever Yusuf does is good. Then everyone is working and writing answers on their papers and there should be quiet but there's shuffling and scratching pencils and sniggers and fingers fiddling and feet tapping and shoes squeaking and whispers that aren't whispers at all and all the noises are bouncing off me.

Some of the children stare at me and I hear the words *wolf* and *savage* floating on the pencil-shaving scented air. Mr Bennett flaps his hand at the mutterers and the words fade away. He puts a chair next to my table and he asks me to start the maths questions and then we can *see where we are*. We're in a cage of a classroom but I don't say that and I scribble my way through the first question and he raises an eyebrow because he seems to like doing that and he nods and then I untangle the next one and he says *good girl* and I burn again but in a good way and Yusuf says *teacher's pet* but he's smiling and I don't think he's said it to be mean.

I get full marks on the maths sheet even though my hand is shaking a bit and Yusuf gives me a shove on the arm and I shove him back but a bit too hard and he falls off his chair. Mr Bennett comes over and says that he'll let me off because it's my first week *ever* but in general try not to knock my classmates to the floor and I worry about the cane but a boy called Harry says a really rude word and he just gets his name written on the board, so maybe there aren't canes at this school like there are in the books I've read.

We do art and science and I am not good at art, but I know the science because it's voltage and that's easy-peasy because I help Dad with the batteries and the generator and the solar panels all the time. It makes my tummy clench when I think about doing the sums with him and making sure we've got enough sunpower for the big lamp in the living room and now when he wakes up he'll hate me and he'll tell me we'll never do any of that ever again.

We get to use tiny little batteries and snappy crocodile wires to make a circuit and light up a bulb, and Yusuf makes a *ding* noise every time we do it. Then there's lunch in a clattering hall that stinks of peas and something worse and the food is strange and disgusting and then there's more football. Yusuf tries to get me to join in a skipping rope game that makes more blood stain the knees of my trousers and I show him an altocumulus and tell him there'll be rain, and when the first fat drops start to fall he *gasps* and tells me I'm a wizard. He tries to get me to show the clouds to more people but they start to crowd around me in a circle and their jumpers blur into a blue sea and I can't find the right words and I can't speak to this many people. I whisper to Yusuf that he should tell them instead but he just rolls his eyes. My skin is itchy and feels wrong on my bones and I can't look at all the eyes staring at me. I stare at my palms instead and look at the criss-cross creases that bloom from points into triangles and stars and maps. Then the bell rings heavy in the cold air. The noise splits the crowd and I breathe in the space they've left behind.

We have English, which is reading a book from the library so I get to go and choose one. It takes me a long time because there's too much choice and too many covers that call to me and too many words I haven't read and too many stories I need to know. A woman in an orange jumper that's just the right fire colour of a fox tells me that I can borrow *five books at a time* and I take off with delight.

When the clock ticks to 3 p.m. it's the end of school, but today it doesn't feel like it was as long and still and I don't feel so flat. I burst into the outdoors with my bundle of borrowed books and my secret in my shoe and I breathe in the rain-soaked air. She's waiting for me and when I reach her Yusuf and a girl called Daisy who played the skipping rope game shout *see you, October* and I can see her smiling and then she goes *oh my God, what has happened to your trousers?*

We go to see Dad and I sit mouse-quiet in the car. This is the very first time since I realised everything was my fault, and I am even more horrible and terrible and evil than I was before because I had fun today and I forgot about what I'd done. I am scared and guilty and we have to stop by the side of the road so I can get out and take big gulps of the car fumes battling with the fresh air and try not to be sick. There have been weeks of cars and hospitals and beeps and too many lights and people talking to me and none of them the right ones or saying the right things and nothing else ever. Every day is a repeat and a loop and I know exactly what will

149

happen every single second but it's still scary to see the tubes and the wires but today when we arrive everything is different.

Today they're going to wake him up.

I haven't got a story for him yet.

And what if he hates me?

What if he hates me?

There are pins in his back and pins in his hips and pins in his arm and he won't be able to walk or really sit up and the doctor says that Dad had an *axial burst fracture* in his spine and I think that sounds beautiful like a shower of stars but what it really means is that he needs a long long time to get better.

I'm not allowed in the room while they pull the tube from his throat and sit him up and tell him where he is and ask him his name, but I'm in the corridor and I can hear snatches of questions and coughs and then I hear something that makes me feel exactly the same as I do when we plunge into the freezing pond.

His voice.

It's a bit croaky and strange and if he were the quad bike I'd be pouring oil into his engine but it's him and he's awake and he's saying my name and so I run in and my arms are around him and I bury my head into his chest and I don't care that he can't hug me back properly because of all the tubes and wires because he's stroking my hair and I don't think he hates me and he's back he's back he's back and we can go home and be wild again and I can leave London and leave *her* and I tell him in an excited jumble of chatter.

She's your mother, October, October. He says it again and again and it's so familiar that for a moment it's like we're far away from the hospital and we're back by the dancing flames of the fire and we're making shadow puppets and watching the night swirl its cloak around us.

But then he turns his head away and coughs and machines beep and a nurse checks screens and she shoos me off the bed and I wait for Dad to say *no no, October, October, stay here with me* but he doesn't and he breathes out *maybe it's time for you to go home with your mother eh, October. I'm so tired* and the deep dark fog rises and mists around me again and it swells to fill the space between us.

He thinks that's my home now. Not our little wooden house painted green and hugged by trees and filled with all the right things and just us two. He's stitching me together with her and London and he's pulling himself away from me because of what I did and he's forgetting how beautiful and wonderful and magical everything was before he fell.

I have to fix this. Something inside me roars and settles and solidifies. All of the stories I've told him while we sat by a smoking fire spitting flames into a midnight sky whirl and spark inside

me and I imagine bottling each and every one and watching their colours swim inside clear glass. They're a magic spell that keeps us together and they're made up of smoke and leaves and scavenged objects and my fizzing imagination and the life we have hidden in the woods. I think of the ring and how excited I was to share its story with him before he fell from the sky. But it's not enough now. It has to be a new story. It has to be the most brilliant potion of them all. Just the right mix of everything. One that reminds him of the smoke and the leaves and the woods and our life. It has to be perfect so he'll forgive me and he'll want me back with him and so he'll remember that it was perfect just me and him. Or I might have to stay in London. Forever. With her.

We go and see Dad again after school on Monday, even though it's a long drive after a very long day and the woman who is my mother still has more work to do and she says she can only really do it in her shed, but she goes to the cafe to tap at her computer and I sit next to Dad and tell him about school. I don't tell him about the screaming and when the world fell to pieces and the library and the feeling of maybe making friends or the clapping games or the jumping over the tangle of rope or that Yusuf and Daisy said I was *cool* or Maryam asking me why my name is October and even when I couldn't answer she said she should be called February and everyone gave themselves their birthday months as names. I'm not sure why I don't tell him. I tell him about getting top marks on the maths paper because it was the same maths we'd used together when we worked out how big the vegetable patches were and how many things we could plant in them. He doesn't say much but he squeezes my hand and then in short broken sentences he tells me how to care for Stig now she's bigger and how to still find stars in a smoggy sky. I can't find the words to tell him that because of me Stig is gone and it feels like the stars are gone too because if I tell him he might say *well what did you expect to happen after what you did?*

155

When the woman who is my mother comes back from the cafe I don't want to leave him and I stomp and crack my knuckles and the pops explode and so do I and I shout.

A nurse sits me down on a chair outside Dad's room and gets me a plastic cup of water that's so cold it makes my brain shriek and stops me shouting. She straightens her blue and white uniform and sits next to me and swings her feet back and forth. She looks at me and says *you can't make all that noise, you know, people are trying to get better* but she doesn't say it in a mean way and she puts her arm around my stiff shoulder and for just that moment I want to be held. I rest my head against her and let myself deflate just a tiny bit and I can hear snatches of the woman who is my mother's words wandering from Dad's room, but his replies are lost to the hiss of machines and the new quiet mew of his voice.

Just so unhappy at home
How can I help her

Stay

No I've never seen her do that at all, not once

Don't know what to do

How can I even start

She

Hates

Me

Would that even work

And I don't know what she's asking about and I don't care because in five minutes I'll be back in the car and back alone with her and back under the crushing London sky.

In the car she says that now I am at school and she is working we'll have to visit Dad once or twice or absolutely at the most three times a week and not every day but that soon he'll be moved to a special recovery hospital and that would be closer and we could go more. A dark thought flashes and it hisses that what if Dad has asked that I don't go as much because he's cross and he hates me and I've broken him and I've broken the links between us and he's going to get better and go back to the woods without me and without the trouble I cause. I ask how long it'll be before I can go home, and something crosses her face but she says *I don't know, October* even though grown-ups are supposed to know things like that and I hate being eleven and no one telling me anything at all.

We stop before an hour and thirty-seven minutes is up. My eyes are closed and I keep them closed because I think we must be in the flashing bright unnatural lights of the service station with its low-slung buildings and thick poisonous air, but she puts a hand on my shoulder and says *quick they close soon* and I open my eyes. We're at the owl rescue and my heart soars but she's saying *just a visit just to see her* and it swirls down to my shoes.

*   *   *

Jeff takes me to Stig's shed. It is cold outside and the sky is white. She is puffed up on a perch and I worry that she's chilly but she looks bigger and fatter and her feathers are beautiful. *Aye she's got her flight feathers coming in all right* says Jeff and he gives a low piercing whistle and Stig moves her head all the way round like owls can do in that strange and magical way and when she sees me I think she knows. *I'm sorry* I whisper through the wire mesh of the shed and my soaring swooping heart cracks again.

Jeff tells us that Stig is happy and healthy and I've done a *flipping good job* and that he hopes she can be part of the wild again when she's big enough, and what they're doing now is rewilding her and that means they're helping her to know that she's an owl and not a person and that humans aren't her friends and how to hunt and how to survive and how to be wild. And I think about my clean jeans and my unmuddied shoes and my pink and white crescent-moon nails and my untangled hair and the clocks that keep my time and I want to be rewilded too.

159

At school Yusuf and I are sent to the library to do our project and I'm a bit worried because Yusuf doesn't seem to want to do any work and I still don't know for sure that there's no cane in Mr Bennett's desk. Yusuf doesn't seem like he's worried at all and he flops down on the beanbag and pulls something out of his pocket and unwraps it. There's a smell like sugar and he passes me a bit of whatever it is and puts the rest in his mouth. I ask him what it is and his mouth hangs open and shows me the whatever it is all chewed up and spitty. *You never even had a Mars bar before* he says, even though there's a lot of food in his mouth. I shake my head no and he rolls his eyes and throws up his hands and says *you haven't lived* but that's stupid because of course I have. *Do you just hunt your own food* he asks and I take a bite of the Mars bar before I answer and it's sweet and delicious and warm, although I think that's because it's been in Yusuf's pocket. I think about telling him we hunt for our food with spears or on horseback or just with our lightning-fast hands and snapping tearing teeth but instead I tell him a bit about the growing tunnel and the once-a-year trips to the village and going to Bill's dairy farm and he sucks the chocolate off his fingers and says *I wish I lived in the woods. But only if there were Mars bars and Coco Pops too.*

When we've eaten the Mars bar I try to fit together the right words to tell Yusuf that we should probably do some work. He is throwing a strange see-through ball with an orange plastic tiger in its belly at the wall and singing a song I don't know because I don't know any of the songs people sing here. He turns to look at me and says *oh yeah don't worry chill out, October* and

161

I don't know how to make myself colder but then he says *by the way what you've got there is a poesy ring.*

His words wipe my face into an expression I can't see and I don't think I've ever had before and he laughs and says *I googled it.* He shrugs. I want to ask what a google is but he's already sweeping on and still throwing the ball at the wall.

So it's like this ring that people gave to each other
Thud
Like a million years ago or the Victorians or something
Thud
And they always had these messages inside
Thud
And they were usually love messages
Thud
He stops here to make a noise like he's being sick
Thud
But sometimes they were just secrets between two people

Thud

So your ring is probably half of a pair that says what
the secret is

Thud

The other one could be anywhere

Thud

Maybe it says where buried treasure is and we'll be
millionaires

And my heart thuds harder than the ball. There's
another ring and it could be buried deep in the soil of
the woods and I feel a tug in my heart pulling me
back to my home.

If I had the other ring I really would have the
perfect story. This is why I haven't been able to find
the story yet. I would have two halves of a whole
and I could tell Dad the story and it would wash away
the blame and glue us back together. I imagine sitting
on his bed in the hospital and showing him the two
rings and telling him a story of the forests and owls
and two people who are like the two sides of a splayed

oak leaf or the two halves of a chestnut husk and he'll remember our woods and me and he'll remember our woods and me and him and that they're not right without each other.

I've got no way to get back to my woods and my fingers twist and itch to search and scavenge and find the story for Dad.

Outside of the library Yusuf is exactly the same as he is inside it, but I am different. He moves around people like he's liquid. They laugh at his jokes and they want him to like them and they ask him to play and he fits into every group like a jigsaw piece slotting into place. Even Harry, who always has his name on the board for using rude words and pushes people over during football, wants Yusuf to be his friend.

I am made of rock. In the woods I could dip through the trees like I was the wind but here my muscles and sinews have hardened and my words come out jagged and sharp. I don't know how to chat and giggle and play and be a part of anything. I've never wanted to before and I've never cared what anyone but Dad thought about me before. I've never needed friends before.

The rest of the school moves around me at a distance and they don't ask so many questions or try to get me to play with them any more. I'm on the very edge of them and I feel like I might fall off.

I look at Yusuf and I feel a sudden lurch of loneliness surrounded by a hundred blue jumpers and thumping footballs.

On Saturday I forget that it's a day you don't go to school and I get up and put on my stupid blue jumper and aching shoes and I sit at the table in the dining room and I eat the eggs on toast that she left out for me and the cold metal shivers my arms. The yolk is dull and flat and nothing like the little golden domes we have in the woods from Bill's chickens. Their yolks burst in a splash of sunshine. These are rubbery greying circles that taste of nothing. Grey grey grey.

She walks in from the garden and her strange looming shed. Her hands are smudged with something black and there's a smell rolling off her skin and it's sharp and rusty and iron-rich. She smiles and says *I love having a short commute* and I don't know what *commute* means so I tuck it away for later because I'm certainly not going to ask her. I shrug and she says *OK pop and get changed and then off we go* and then I realise it's not a school day and I think she's going to bundle me in the car for the miles of motorway so I start to pack my new library books because reading in the car doesn't make me feel sick any more and I want to race through the chapters so I can get a new book or five on Monday.

For weeks my path has been straight across the gritty grey pavement and into the front seat and back again except for the trudge up the road to school and when we went on the Underground and everything went black. I don't even look side to side. There's no point. It's all the same thing repeated over and over and over again. Grey. House. School. Grey. School. House. School. Grey. House. All under a tremblingly close and heavy sky.

Grey grey grey.

But we don't get in the car.

We're going on an adventure.

These are the same words she used before and panic catches my heart. Her words sound like a book I read when I was very small and maybe she even read it to me. But that was an adventure in the wild through the sticky mud and the wet rivers and this is a plod along cold concrete that seeps its damp into my boots and what if we're going underground again even though she promised me we wouldn't. Then all of a sudden we stop and we stand under a glass and plastic shelter until a huge red bus roars and squeals and hisses open its doors. She *bips* something flat from her pocket on to a yellow circle and then says something to the driver that I don't catch and he nods and I follow her up some helter-skelter stairs and before we can even sit down we're lurching off and I'm flying towards a window.

She catches me before I hit the glass or the floor or maybe both and hoists me on to a seat with prickly patterned fabric. I grip the sides so tightly that my knuckles burst white against my skin. I try to disappear into a story about a girl flying a rocket all around the Earth in one long looping circle, but the noises are pressing into me again and my brain won't work.

We whizz past buildings that get taller and taller. The angles all shift and some are rounded and fat and some are skinny and spiky and it's all a bit like the art or sculptures I've seen in my books and not like buildings at all.

The bus takes what feels like a long time, but the light doesn't change so maybe it's quick as a flash. She points at things out of the window and she says their names but I don't let the words stick in my brain. Then she presses a little red button and there's a *ding* and we're picking our way down the terrible helter-skelter but I don't fall. The doors hiss open and she takes my hand and I don't have time to pull away before we're off the bus and there is an explosion of people and noise and I'm terrified.

I don't let go of her hand because I can feel myself

being washed away and turned and tumbled through the waves and seas and oceans of people who walk and stroll and jog and run and there are huge prams with wheels as big as a tractor's and skinny dogs on leads and hairy dogs barking and jumping and children shouting and laughing and crying and it's like all the stories I've ever read have come tumbling out of my head and their characters are spilling and spreading around me.

She pulls me *p---o---p* like a cork from a bottle and we're moving through the crowd as if it wasn't even there at all and we spiral through the streets and it's a blur and then she says *look* and the world has

o   p   e   n   e   d   up.

I can smell something that isn't cars and people and it's a salt-fresh brackish tang and the sound of water.

The River Thames. Wide and flat and still grey but pecked by free-flying birds and trying to glitter in the pale November light. She tells me that the Thames is a tidal river and it washes in and out and every time it brings something new and takes something else away with it.

Its tide laps at the shore like a tired dog and it ripples and sways like I've always imagined the sea. She takes me down some steps and on to a stone-speckled grey-sand shore that stretches and bends until it runs out of sight.

There's a space here that I have been trying to find ever since my horrible birthday. There are still buildings on the banks but they feel pushed back by the open air and the bright glass of the water. I breathe out and I laugh and I can see the sound painted cold in the frosty air. I spread my arms out wide and feel the wind with my fingertips, and she looks at me and whispers *he said you'd like this* and I know she means Dad.

There are people on the shore but not many because it's so cold and damp, but I don't care about that and it doesn't seem like they do either. They're dressed in waterproofs and heavy boots and their hoods are pulled up against the wind. They're not much more than dark shapes outlined against the empty sky and it's impossible to see if they're old or young or men or women or even human beings at all. There's definitely a dog and he's slick with water and covered in sand and mud and he throws himself into the river after floating branches and barks his head off. The dark shapes are bent over and scrabbling in the sand and some of them have great long metal rods that beep. When I hear that I feel a scrunch in my chest because that sound is Dad's new heartbeat.

Mudlarks.

I look up and she says it again. *They're mudlarks. They search for treasure here.*

Mudlarks.

Things from the wild and from nature and from the earth and from the sky. Searching for treasure and scraps of stories washed up and washed away again by the iron-grey tide. Forever changing into something new and offering something different with every pull of the moon. The smog of the city lifts up a tiny little infinitesimal shred of itself because maybe this is where stories can end up. Maybe this is where rings end up. A dizzy rush is swirling up from my tummy and it tingles in my fingers. It feels fizzy and unusual and like something from long ago but new and exciting at the same time. The buzz of stories and searching and finding the old and making the new.

I keep staring at the mudlarks and their buckets and their little spades and their beeping machines, which the woman who is my mother says are *metal detectors*. She turns a stone over in her hand and holds it flat in her palm and shows me how it was once glass that the water has smoothed and shaped into a gem. It looks just like the magic stones I found in the woods and slipped under Dad's pillow in hospital. I start to feel the woods and the water stitching themselves together in my mind and the story of the stones starts to spin again in my brain. The wolfboy and his love met in the wilds of the woods. He was thrown to the animals in the frost-dashed dark and torn away from her with only the thin gold band to remember her by and no magic in the world strong enough to pull them back together. Her matching ring with its answering secret and this one bright gem spilled from the side of a boat as she sailed through London to escape. She cast away the things he had given her so no one could take them from her and because she always knew they would find their way back to each other. It still broke her heart and then she slipped into the tangle of streets to hide from people who wanted to throw her to the wolves too.

The woman who is my mother puts the glass gem into my hand and tells me that when she was my age she lived by the sea and she was a scavenger and a picker-upper because every little thing she found would go into her pocket. She says she still swoops when she sees something glinting and beautiful and that when she moved to London she could comb the river foreshore here just like when she was young and it gave her a wildness and a freedom that was missing from the maze of streets. She says that when I was tiny and could only just walk I was like a magpie and I'd pick up everything I found and cry if it was taken away from me even if it was just a pebble. And I want to say I'm still like that and she'd know this if she hadn't left us but she turns to me and her eyes are bright and she says *we're not a million miles apart, October* and I can feel my face harden.

We stop talking and we walk down the muddy sand

and I skim stones across the flat water and watch the mudlarkers from the corner of my eye.

We sit on damp rocks that dust our trousers with sand and she takes a plastic flask from her bag and we drink hot chocolate from cups that fit neatly on to its lid. The chocolate steams and scents the air and then she drops fluffy pink and white pillows into the cups and they melt into a sugary sticky goo and I scoop some on to my finger because it's so delicious and this is my first ever hot chocolate that wasn't in a book.

I can see the mudlarks crowding round something that catches the pale light and it could be a cursed coin or a magic key or a necklace jointed with jewels or a pirate's gold tooth or a ring with a secret message. We watch birds swooping down for fish and eels. A cormorant throws back its head and swallows one whole and I see every wiggle and gulp as the eel slips down its long neck. It's all so different and so new but I'm not dry-mouthed and terrified for the first time in forever, and for a split second or maybe even a whole second I can feel something like hope.

There is a wildness here and there are tales to tell. I can find the matching ring and I can tell its most perfect story to Dad and it'll stitch us together again and everything will be OK. I can fix this. My eyes start to skim and scan and flutter across the surface of the mudflats. It's very different to the familiar midnight black and conker brown of the mud in the woods and it's like someone has switched around all the colours in my vision. I sweep my eyes back and forth hoping for a glimpse of glitter or the sparkle of a something shining in the weak winter sun. But I can't get to grips with the new ground and rain starts to spit from the sky and when I'm soaked to the bone she leads me away.

The bus home is too loud and it smells like something hot and greasy but I sit at the front on the top floor by the huge glass windowscreen and we drive into the darkness. I am the captain of a space-age pirate ship returning from a great treasure-seeking adventure in a far-flung star-speckled corner of the Milky Way and we have to battle crowds of aliens who whirl and shout and crowd and shoot their ray guns at us and we very nearly tumble out of the sky until I press the secret red button and we are jerked and boosted and we lurch and then the hidden tubes *hissssss* the release of an alien-stunning gas and open the doors at the same time and we can jump off the spaceship and land safely on our home planet.

In my head there are six words chasing each other through my brain.

I want to be a mudlark.

I still hate London, and spaceship buses and riverbirds and treasure hunting can't change that at all. The light is all wrong here. The sounds and smells are wrong. The ground and the air and the sky are wrong wrong wrong. They belong to her and I don't want to be like her, but I can't stop thinking about the pull of the tide and the sparkle of things

waiting to be found. A ring waiting to be found. A
story waiting to be told.

There is a little spark of something that wasn't here
before and I keep it tucked tight inside me, just like
the secret in my pocket.

Dad has been moved to his new hospital, and the next day we go and see him. It's not an hour and thirty-seven minutes away this time. It's twenty-nine minutes in the car and it's amazing and brilliant and all the wonderful words because Dad is close to me even if that is still measured in miles at the moment and it's also terrible and bad and awful and all the spiky bitter words because trapping Dad in a city is the wrongest thing in the world.

He has his own little room and the floors are pale pink like the very first petals of a wild flower. He has a TV and a fridge and a framed painting of an empty field and it's like someone has tried to make it like a home but it's not anything like our home and it's probably not much like anyone's home. He is sitting up in a bed just like the one in the other hospital and when he sees me he throws his arms out wide and he says my name twice so loudly that my heart lifts and a nurse pokes his head round the door.

It's almost right being back with Dad, even though the floor is pink and even though the window looks out on to buildings and cranes and even though everything smells sharp and strange. The woman who is my mother melts away and out of the room and we sit together and play Snap and a game called Uno that one of the nurses lends us and another one called Mouse Trap, which I'm not keen on at first because I don't want to trap a mouse but it's just a little plastic one and I forget that I don't like the idea because it's fun.

The shadows stretch and I know that I'm going to have to leave soon, but I want to stay and I ask if I can have a room here. I think about the ring story that I've

been trying to piece together and stitch into something new and special enough to fix what's happened
and I open my mouth to try to fling out a few words
because maybe if I start then it will take its own
shape. But then he says *your mother will be back soon*
and my face darkens to a thundercloud and he says
Oh October, October, you have to give her a chance. He
strokes my cheek and his finger is smooth like he's
shedding the forest from his skin like a snake and I
think of the smashed leveret and the broken plates
and the trip to see the mudlarks and the hot chocolate
and then I think of Stig in her wire-roofed prison
being taunted by the open sky and I explode and I
shout and I tell him what she did with our owl and
the story of the ring dissolves.

The nurse comes running in again, but I don't
even notice because I'm too shocked by Dad. He is
holding out his soft new hand to me but I'm moving
away from him and towards the door and towards
I don't know what because he's just told me it was *for
the best.*

Leaving Stig in a cage with strangers is *for the best*.

And I know he thinks leaving me here trapped under a London sky with the woman who is my mother is *for the best too*.

He's going to leave me here.

On Monday I am still cross and furious and the mudlark visit magic that sparked a little between me and the woman who is my mother has rubbed away and the silence is back and now it stretches all the way to Dad too.

But in the library at school I can't help it and I show off my new word to Yusuf. I drop it and let it soar.

Mudlark.

Yusuf whistles and I wish I could do that too. I want to ask him to teach me, but we've only got half an hour before break and Mr Bennett wants to see some *signs of progress* today, which Yusuf says means we have to show him some actual work.

Yusuf sits at the computer that I don't know how to use and types the word on to the screen. He knows exactly where all the letters on the keyboard are and his fingers dance across them. He speaks even faster than usual and he's reading phrases and words and facts that have magically appeared.

Mudlarking was a job. A horrible job. In a horrible time.

Children with no money scavenged the shores of the Thames to find treasure to stay alive. Sometimes they found coins. Sometimes they found rubbish. Sometimes they found bones and bodies and decay. Sometimes they found something that would make them rich.

They didn't have to work in the soot-dusted air of a factory or be stuffed up into the darkness of a chimney or sweat in the black of a coal pit for pennies that barely put bread on the table. They could be outside. They could choose when to work. They could keep what they found.

It was a kind of freedom.

Yusuf shows me a drawing of a pair of mudlarks. They are standing in the shallow waters of the river and their feet are scribbled with mud. Their hair is wild pencil streaks and their faces are wild.

Wild in London.

And it's like there's a hole in history and I'm looking right through it and they're looking back at me and it's a mirror and a reflection and it's a way to fit everything together.

We can hunt for treasure breathes Yusuf, and I nod my head so hard he warns me that it might fall off.

We can hunt for the ring.

*F*ollow *my lead* Yusuf whispers in my ear when
the last bell rings. *Which one's your mum?* I
clench my fists when he says that because that's not
the right word for her but I don't want to tell him that
so I just point and hiss *don't mention the word
mudlarking* because I don't want her to think I'm like
her. He scampers off towards her and I run too
because I don't quite trust whatever Yusuf might do,
and I'm right because when I get there he's being nice
to her. He's talking about *history* and *top of the class*
and *a trip* and *big brother will come* and *museums are
so educational aren't they* and he's smiling his big smile
with all the teeth and the woman who is my mother

186

is smiling too. She is saying how *that sounds lovely of course* and *when were you thinking* and when he answers she pauses and looks at me and says *oh Saturday is when October goes to see her dad* and I think of lonely Stig and *it's for the best* and the heart sting of that sentence and I find myself saying

I don't want to go this week.

On Saturday I put on my raggedy old trousers, which still smell like woodsmoke because I won't let her wash them, and a big red knitted jumper. It's so thick that my coat will barely stretch to do up over it but when she says *oh we need to get you a bigger coat* I ignore her because this one is just fine and it has pockets in all the right places and there's a special little zippy one just for the ring. All the other new clothes she's bought me are still in their bags lined up against the walls of my room. I haven't even looked at them, because they're not mine, not really. I pack my coat pockets with essentials like apples and tissues and rubber bands and a tiny penknife that Dad gave me when I was eight and old enough and the little trowel from my treasure box and I am a mudlark from all the way back through loops of time and I'm ready for a day at work in the wilds of the water and to find treasure.

Yusuf and his brother, Ibi, ring the doorbell at exactly ten o'clock and I answer the door, which is the first time I've ever done that. The woman who is my mother comes to the door too and she starts talking to Ibi about things like buses and times and being responsible, which is ridiculous because Ibi is eighteen and has his own car and a job after college and a girlfriend called Yasmin who gives Yusuf sweets. Ibi nods and says all the right things and he nods at me and says *all right, October* and I don't know what to say back. Yusuf shoves him and says *dude, I told you she only speaks wolf* and Ibi shoves him back and says *I do apologise for my brother we think he must be missing the plumbing between his brain and his mouth it's tragic really* and the woman who is my mother laughs and asks me if I have everything I need but I don't answer her either so maybe Ibi thinks I really am just a wolfspeaker.

We get the bus again and I'm almost used to the strange lurches and jerks and hisses and squeals by the time we get off. Yusuf produces two Mars bars from his pocket and he gives one to me. Ibi rolls his eyes and says Yusuf's teeth will rot right out of his head, which is exactly what Dad says about sugar.

We are in a different place to before. Yusuf is looking at his phone and following a circle that moves along the mapped streets as we walk. I can't stop staring at it. My scraps of maps and veiny pencil pictures of the woods seem so babyish. Yusuf says *OK so scavenging first then we'll do the museum*. He yawns when he says *museum*, even though it was his idea and he found it on the internet. A museum right by the river filled with things people had found in the water and in the mud. I can feel the excitement sparking in my skin.

The tide is out, which means the flat muddy sand is uncovered and the water has washed up some of its stories and washed away others. We go down steps slippery with spray and river weed and plunge on to the foreshore. Yusuf has a blue plastic spade and I have my little trowel. Yusuf looks a bit embarrassed about his spade and he says something about the beach and building sandcastles when he was little and I think that sounds amazing. I've never been to the beach, except in books. I realise too late that neither of us has a bucket for our treasure but both our coats have big pockets.

Ibi takes a book out of his coat and tries to find somewhere to sit. Everything is wet and everything smells like dead water and old mud. He shakes his head and mutters darkly and then tells us he's going to sit on a bench on the river path and if we dare drown then he'll kill us anyway.

Yusuf waves him off cheerily and starts to dig with his little plastic spade. Fat wet lumps of sand fly and thump and spit. I walk up and down the sinking ground with breath pluming white and I imagine those mudlark children with no shoes or coats freezing in the frost and desperate to find something that will set them free. I scan the mud and sometimes I flip over a stone if something sparkles, but this is harder than hunting in the woods. My eyes were eagle there but here the landscape is all different and I can't grip on. There's no change to the texture of the mud and everything looks the same.

Yusuf is still digging madly. He shouts every five seconds that he's found something and then follows it with *oh no don't worry*. I close my eyes and take a deep breath and try to turn my brain off and throw all the thoughts out of my mind, just like I do when I scavenge in the woods. I pour away Stig and the trees and handfuls of fury and my fight with Dad and lumps of worry. I listen to the pull and lap of the water and the call of the riverbirds and the way the wind twists around the buildings and flings itself into the wide sky. I open my eyes and the winter sun bounces off the water and everything is sharper.

The mud printed with the shape of the water and the drag of the tide. The mud that's pulled and pressed with the weight of something else. The stones that fan out and the stones that huddle tightly. I see the shape of the river and the sky and the ground.

I feel this new world with my fingertips. I am a treasure hunter again. I find a clay pipe and I show it to Yusuf and he doesn't look very impressed, until he finds one too and then he whoops with delight and the sound fills the sky and Ibi's head appears over a wall at the top of the steps and he checks we're not drowning.

We don't find much more after the clay pipes and our hands start to freeze and Yusuf says his might fall off. He is jumping with ideas and saying things like *imagine if we found gold and jewels* and *how cool would it be if we found a skeleton* and *do you think my mum would let me have a real skeleton in my bedroom* like I might know the answer. In my head I can see a moment unfolding itself like a pop-up book. A glint of gold in the mud. Holding the perfect circle up to the sky like a second sun. Fitting together the story and running to tell Dad every beautiful detail and him smiling and telling me he loves me and I'm going back home home home with him.

I put my hands in my pockets, along with the clay pipe and a little circle that could be a coin or could be a stone washed smooth. Yusuf is taking it in turns to blow on his hands and take bites of his Mars bar, so I do the same and the chocolate warms my tummy. I lick the strands of sticky golden goo that Yusuf says is *caramel* from my fingers and taste sugar and river. Yusuf keeps complaining that his hands are going to fall off from the cold, but I don't want to leave just yet because what if I miss the ring and it's washed away with the tide and I never find it? The cold suddenly seeps into the hollows of my bones at the thought and I start to scan again, but Yusuf is already scampering towards the steps and shouting about going somewhere else next.

We collect Ibi, who looks quite grateful not to be sitting on the bench any more because it's covered in a frost dust, and we walk down a narrow cobbled street that's like it's from olden times. I've seen

194

enough streets in London to know that they're mostly big fat flat boring grey squares all glued together, but these are amazing. The cobbles are different sizes and when I walk over the top of them I can feel their domed shape through my boots. They're higgledy and piggledy in a way I didn't think London could be and I can almost hear the echo of horses' hoofs clip-clopping from a hundred years ago.

The museum is in an old warehouse that used to be used to store things delivered by the big boats on the Thames, or maybe to put things on to those boats. The windows are huge and you can see flashes of the river sweeping past so it's a bit like being on a ship although I've never been on a ship, except in books. There is a woman with short spiky purple hair reading a book behind a desk as we walk in and she doesn't look up from the pages except to wave her hand.

Ibi immediately sits down on a chair that isn't icy and starts to read again. Yusuf and I wander through the echoing room towards huge glass cases at the back. They remind me of Snow White's coffin, but instead of a dead princess they're filled with treasure.

Clay pipes and pottery. Coins and looping chains of necklaces. Black lumps that are labelled as shoes and hats. White shards of bone. Metal cups. A gold tooth. Combs. Tiny naked china dolls with painted smiles and staring eyes. Rings with twisted metal patterns snaking their metal.

Yusuf is tugging my sleeve. *It says the mud is … is* his voice trips over the next word on the sign. *Anaerobic* I say *anna-roh-bic*. He nods. *Yeah that it's anna-roh-bic and that means no oxygen in the mud and that means things are preserved just as when they went in*. I look at the shoes and the hats and I'm not convinced but the gold tooth is perfect and it looks like it could be popped straight back into the mouth of a pirate.

There's a printed story of a mudlark and it's the saddest thing I've ever read. A little boy. Six or seven. No shoes and no coat. Ten dead siblings and two dead parents and no one to buy him food or make him warm socks or tell him to tidy up. Twice a day when the moon's tug pulled the tide away he would hunt and scavenge for anything he could find for hours and hours until the water started to curl around his ankles. Pockets bulging with scraps and nuggets. Somethings and nothings. And that's how they found him two hundred years later when the water dragged his story to the shore. A skinny boy skeleton still dressed and with pockets full of finds. Maybe he fell asleep or maybe he slipped or maybe he just couldn't carry on. Nobody noticed he'd disappeared under the water one day. No one knew his name so they called him Tom. Tom from the Thames.

No one had even missed him.

No one planted trees on his birthday or carved him a wooden chest for his treasures or bought him soft pyjamas stitched with foxes.

Yusuf pulls his clay pipe out of his pocket and he's rubbing the city silt from its curves and I pull myself back to the present and leave Tom in the past. I try to match my strange little coin with anything behind the glass. Yusuf is busy holding his pipe up to the light and wondering whether it's worth a hundred pounds or a million pounds when a voice cuts through the dusty air.

Where did you get that?

It's the woman from behind the desk except she's not behind the desk any more and she's standing in front of us with her hands on her hips and Yusuf is making the same face he makes when Mr Bennett asks him where his Reading Record is. He isn't making any sounds so I tell her it's from the foreshore of the river and that we're *mudlarks* and she stares at me and I don't think I should have said a word.

It turns out that you're not allowed to call yourself a mudlark and then just be a mudlark because there are *rules* and I think this is really stupid and I tell the museum woman that and she goes a bit pink and I know I must have been rude because Yusuf pinches my arm.

You're meant to have special permission just to search on the foreshore and without it you can't dig or scrape the surface and to be an official *mudlark* you need an even more special permission and it costs lots of money and even then you're not allowed to keep anything you find if it might be *important*. It belongs to The City. London gobbles up the good. I hate it. Rules and boundaries and laws and money and taking away things that belong to other people.

The woman says we're lucky we're not in more trouble, then she looks at our finds. I keep the ring in the tiny secret zippy pocket inside my coat because otherwise she might not believe me that I found it a million miles away and she might try to take it and put it in a glass coffin and only let me visit it some-times with permission.

The woman asks us why we're mudlarking. For *education* says Yusuf fiercely, and she looks a bit embarrassed and fiddles with the cuffs of her jumper. *Show me again what you have* she says and she looks at the clay pipes and tells us they're Victorian and that lots of people smoked pipes back then and that these ones probably belonged to poorer people because they're plain and smooth. She points to a pipe in a glass case and it's carved and shaped in intricate patterns that I long to run my fingers over. Yusuf asks if our pipes are valuable and she laughs and says no and he deflates with disappointment. She takes the little coin from my hand and turns it over so it catches the light. *It's a token for the ferry. Pay the ferryman to cross the river. Maybe it was dropped overboard or maybe it was in the pocket of somebody who ended up in the water. The river is full of stories like that.*

Yusuf is extremely impressed that my token might have come from a dead person and he asks questions at the speed of light and his excitement is whirling around me but I am a thundercloud. We can't scavenge in this stupid city. The disappointment curls around me like smoke.

We get the bus home and the sadness and the river smell roll off me in waves. Even Yusuf is quiet, except for chewing on pieces of chocolate-covered toffee that he produces from a damp pocket and offers round. I am cold and I am wet and I am muddy and these things usually make me happy but today misery is soaked into my bones and I can't shake it off.

Our adventure is over before it's begun. We'll never

find another ring and I won't find the other half of the secret and I'll have no more windswept wild moments in the flat open space of the river and I won't find the shape of a story to tell Dad.

When I walk in the door I don't take my muddy boots off and I trail the history of the Thames through the house and I drip water that tingles with stories and I smear mud that holds secrets. The woman who is my mother barks at me to *take off those boots* and it's the first time she's used a voice of steel and the weight of the day presses down too hard and I cry and her voice softens into *oh my darling*.

She runs me a bath. It's not the same as our fat-bellied tub but it swirls the air with steam and she pours something that smells like wild bluebells into the water and it blooms in a violet foam. I sink under the water and it soaks the sadness from my bones, and in the heat and the steam and the flower scent and the bubbles I feel a little bit better.

She sits outside the bathroom door. I can see the shape of her shadow creeping under the gap between floor and door, but I don't shout at her to go away or to leave me alone. She hums a tune that sounds like something from far away in my memory and I hum a little bit of it to see if I'm right but I keep the music inside my head because I don't want her to know. Then she tells me a story.

I'm usually the one who tells stories.

Even Dad doesn't tell me stories.

I am swept away by the words and the magic and the secrets and the bubbles flatten and the water stops steaming and I'm a world away. A little girl on a windswept beach searching for shells and bones and gemstones. A little girl with the salt-spray of sea in her hair finding treasures and making them into something new. She sewed and glued and stitched and hammered and twisted until these old scraps were beautiful. Sea glass became a ring and shells were strung into necklaces and she'd give them to anyone who needed a little bit of kindness. The girl grew up and up, but she kept searching and making and one day she made the most beautiful fox from driftwood to put by the bed of someone magical, to watch over them while they slept.

When I get out of the bath and go to my bedroom I see the pyjamas she bought me still folded neatly on my little desk. I trace the stitching and find tiny trees and badgers as well as foxes, and they have pockets. This time I put them on and I slip the ring into the pocket that sits right by my heart.

We order pizza for tea. I've never eaten pizza and I've never ordered food before and she shows me how to click through options on her flat phone and I choose pineapple because we have that at home in tins sometimes and I choose mushroom because we grow those and then I choose olives and artichokes because I've never had those before and after a moment I add spinach because it's good for you. She raises her eyebrows but she doesn't say anything, and when the doorbell rings the pizza is here just like magic and I love all of my toppings except for the spinach because it gets all tangled in my teeth.

I don't go straight up to my room after supper like

I normally do, and she gets out some wool and knitting needles and puts on the television, which I've never watched before. The colours feel a bit too bright for my eyes and I have to look at the wall behind the TV a lot and the sound is definitely too loud but I try to follow the story anyway. Her pointed needles click and clack and dip and dance and the colours spin from string into something new. When there's a break for something called *adverts*, which is when the sound gets even louder and the TV shows you loads of weird things it thinks you need, she watches a dancing mop whirling across the screen and she wraps the seaweedy strands of wool around her needles and asks *what happened today, October, did you fall out with Yusuf?*

I don't know what to say because if I tell her she might think I like her but if I keep quiet then she might be cross with Yusuf and I don't want that either. So I string together choppy sentences about searching and scavenging and looking for treasure and the museum and being told off and not being able to search any more even though it was for something very special and never being able to find treasure here. I don't say that the special thing for me is to find the rest of the ring's secret message, and she doesn't ask.

She puts her hand out to stroke my bath-wet hair and I pull away and her hand hangs. *Do you want to see some treasure from the story I told you* she says and her voice is a hopeful whisper and I look at her hand folding itself back on to her lap and I nod.

We go to her looming shed in the pretend garden. She unlocks the door with a flash of a silver key and a new world opens up. The air is iron and fire. A huge worktable is cluttered with jars of gems and glass and strange metal machines that I've never seen before, and there are wooden drawers spilling over with metal and wire and tools. I slide one open and gemstones wink.

She opens a box and shows me a silver ring with a diamond perched on the top like a flake of ice on a mountain. *It's an engagement ring for someone who wants to ask someone else to marry them. I made it exactly how they wanted it. The stone belonged to a necklace his grandmother used to wear.*

She makes these treasures. She takes the old and the new and turns them into something else. She shows me more and there is a blowtorch to melt metal into just the right shape and pliers to twist and turn it into silver chains that slip through my fingers like snakes and earrings that are seeded with tiny dots of colour and there are perfect circles of rings that are her favourite to make. They're in black velvet boxes that feel like a rabbit's fur and I stroke them and I think about telling her about my poesy ring but then I remember Stig and I keep my mouth closed tight.

These treasures all have homes to go to and they'll be sent out in parcels and be gone forever. I want to find my own treasures more than anything and my heart bumps against my ribs in disappointment and maybe she gets it because she squeezes my shoulder but so gently that it's like the wind brushing my skin.

In my white bedroom I carefully put my dead man's ferry token and clay pipe into my treasure box, and I am surrounded by stories and my own is falling apart.

The next morning there are some pieces of paper on my plate instead of eggs. My eyes are sleepdusted and heavy and I have to rub them to wake them up before I can read the pages properly.

Mudlarks.

Club.   Junior.
Thames.
Permit.

Words that bounce and words that howl and words that sing.

I, October Holt, have applied to be a Junior Mudlark with Tide and Thames Mudlarking Society.

In the space where it says *parent/guardian signature* she has signed her name with thick blue ink.

There's a *condition*.

Of course there's a condition.

It could never be simple.

Nothing here is.

Once I'm an Official Mudlark, I have to agree to go and see Dad again.

I grumble and groan and mutter and then I agree because I get to go mudlarking first and maybe just maybe I might find the ring and then I can have something for Dad.

She magics the mudlarking forms back into the computer with a flat black box called a *scanner* and with a click and a *whoosh* they've arrived miles away in a different computer and she says you can send words all over the world if you wanted to and I want to talk to people in Australia and Africa and Antarctica and America and I'm only on the As before I remember I don't know anyone there.

At school it's the *last week before the holidays*, which means we get to watch quite a lot of films that everyone else knows all the words to and I've never seen a film before and they're brilliant and loud and I sink into a story about a girl whose parents are turned into pigs by a witch who wants to steal her name. Mr Bennett says we have to at least do a bit of work and he gives us maths that ties me up in knots and I work so hard to unpick the problems that for the very first time the bell doesn't make me jump out of my skin and leave my skeleton behind on my chair We make holiday cards, and my reindeer card for Dad looks more like an ill cat in a spiky hat but Yusuf says

very kindly that it's *artistic*. We make paper snowflakes and I snip and chop and I don't quite believe
what will happen until I unfold the paper and see the
lace pattern peeping through. Yusuf and Maryam
make hundreds and they're just like real snowflakes
because not one is the same as the last and we string
them from the ceiling of the classroom and it looks
like the outside is inside and like winter is a special
sort of spell.

I write down the words that Yusuf needs to type
into his computer so that he can join the Tide and
Thames Mudlarking club too, because we are
sidekicks and a pair
and secret-finders
and I think he's
my friend.
Yusuf is
bouncy and
giddy and
fizzy with the
excitement of

being an Official Mudlark and he wants us to get hats and T-shirts and badges and I'm not sure I like that idea much but he doesn't leave the space for my words so I just listen and his excitement starts to spread and bloom and blossom until it's wrapping itself around me too and I jump up and down with him in the playground. *We can go every day in the holidays can't we* he says and his words go up and down with every jump.

The school term ends with an assembly where everybody sings songs without needing to read the words and I have to keep quiet until the same words start to catch in my brain and I whisper them into the swelling voices that reach up to the roof.

*T*he river washes up its secrets.

The river washes away its secrets.

Every tide tells you a different story.

Twice a day every day the river pulls back and shows you something new.

The woman talking is standing on the foreshore wearing black welly boots with a thousand layers of mud. My wellies are brand new and bright red and too shiny. They were an early Christmas present because my yellow boots were cracked and split and one of the toes fell off when I put them on and the woman who is my mother said *no way are you wearing those* even though I still wanted to. Yusuf is wearing green boots that have faded dinosaurs on them and when I saw the little stegosauruses I said I liked them and he said *oh shut up they still fit so I'm stuck with them* and I didn't understand and I wanted my boots to have dinosaurs on them too.

The woman telling the story of the tides is called Kate and she has a ring in her nose like a bull and I think I might like one of those too. She is in charge of the Junior Mudlarks, which so far is just me and Yusuf and a girl called Tilly who doesn't speak very much and has her hair in two plaits that are so long she can tuck them into her trousers which she does every time we kneel down which is a lot.

Kate is a hawk. Her eyes sweep and scan and she swoops. She holds up a black lump and then she shakes it and it rattles. *Little bell for cattle* she says. *Farmers would bring their livestock on boats and sometimes they'd fall in and drown. I've found a cow skull before* and she shakes the lump again and says *that's a three-hundred-year-old pea in there.* Yusuf sticks out his tongue and whispers *bet it doesn't taste any worse than a new pea* but I like peas so I tell him to be quiet and I listen to Kate.

She teaches us how to search and how to record our finds in notebooks and how not to disturb the riverbed before the water pulls its cold blanket over it. We aren't allowed to dig very deep and she says if we do then we're *out*. She looks at Yusuf when she says this, and he grins and salutes her with his trowel.

Scavenging feels like freedom. I am a mudlarker child sprung from history. I am a wild animal skulking and prowling for food. I am a pirate hunting for treasure. I am a detective on the search for clues. I sink into the rhythm of the search and it feels so new and yet so familiar. The ground is clay and mud and river water and stones, not soil and roots and leaves and sedge. The air is city-stained and not muddled with the wild but my eyes scan and my fingers reach

219

and I'm so lost in the hunt that I lose all time and everything around me melts into a jumble. My eyes are sharp only for finds and the stories they bring.

I don't find a ring. There is no glimmer of gold in this tide and I am burned by disappointment, but only around my edges. In my bucket I have a black Roman coin and two broken clay pipes and a shard of pottery and another ferry token and my absolute favourite, which is a key. It is rusted orange and one end is round in a curlicued circle and the other has thick teeth ready to bite a lock open. It could open a cupboard that has a portal to another world or a box that contains a magic spell or it could release a spirit trapped in a chest or open a castle lost forever under the iron water of the river.

I almost don't tell Kate about the key in case she takes it away because she said anything of *interest* has to go to a museum but I remember her rules and I remember what she said about being *out* and I remember that every time the tide washes away and washes back it brings new finds and I don't want to miss a single one. I show her my other finds first and she makes some notes and she holds up the pottery to the wintery light and says *oh now this is bone!* And I look more closely and she runs her fingers along the cracks in the little sliver of skeleton and says it probably belongs to a cow or a sheep and I'm not sure if I'm disappointed or relieved that it's not human. It's been washed white by the water and it glows against her palm and it's another piece of a story. I show her the key and she says it's Victorian and she found one just last week and *isn't it amazing* to think of all the things they might unlock and I nod and I can hardly catch my breath as she hands it back and winks.

It's my best treasure since leaving the woods.

Yusuf finds a trainer that is definitely not Victorian and it smells like a rat might have been living in it but he puts it in his bucket anyway. He shows me a ferry token and another clay pipe and a coin that is older and more beautiful than mine because it has the raised outline of a wing-flapping bird on it and for a moment I'm jealous.

I didn't find what I was looking for but next time there will be new stories.

When I get home I have a bath and the fresh water muddies itself into the grey river. When I am clean I put the fragments of lives in a line on my little desk and I think about all of the moments they make up. I still can't shake stories loose from my head but I feel a little bit closer.

Yusuf wants us to mudlark every single day but the Tide and Thames club only meets on Sundays and it doesn't meet up over Christmas, and so we scavenge in the park near school instead. Yusuf finds seventeen bottle caps and a broken pen and I find shattered blue glass and food wrappers and plastic bags. I touch the sea-stained glass gently but it doesn't tell me a story and it's sharp beneath the soft pad of my finger so I pull away.

Yusuf has given up searching and he's sitting on a wooden bench blowing his air into fiery dragon breath and arranging his bottle caps into the shape of a Y next to him. He shuffles them all together and makes a circle with them and it's an O for me and it's made from lots of *little Os so it's like double your letter*. I sit down and he scatters the caps and starts building more of the alphabet and I sniff the air. Yusuf shoves me and mutters *weird, man* but I look up at the sky and the clouds roll dark and fat. *Snow* I say. Yusuf looks up too and squints into the empty air and shakes his head, but I catch the smell again and I hold out my hand.

Snow.

We twirl through the falling flakes as they lay a thick blanket over the stubbly grey-green grass and curl up along tree branches. I stick out my tongue and taste the winter.

The woman who is my mother doesn't change her mind.

I have to go and see Dad.

I've been nervous about seeing Dad every single time since we left the woods because of the foggy cloak of guilt that settled on my shoulders. But I've never been cross with Dad, except for the time he ate the very last tin of sticky baked beans when I'd wanted them for my lunch, and even then the crossness slid away before it could settle.

This is different.

He took her side.

We used to be stuck on the same side with our

edges all glued together and nothing could wriggle and slither its way between us.

Now our seams are coming apart and it's like he's pulling the threads.

He's in a chair when we arrive and it's a bit like the world has tilted because he's been lying on his back for so long that the angle of him is all wrong and strange. Tipped up straight he looks skinny and like all his colour must have swirled down from his head and is hiding in his socks.

The nurse on the way in told us he still can't stand up on his own yet but that even sitting is *amazing* and she said it like Dad was a baby and it made me hiss.

Dad is wearing soft trousers and a T-shirt that I've never seen before. He belongs in wood-worn overalls with faded knees and heavy boots that scatter mud with every step. He holds out his hand to me and I'm still very cross with him but I have to try hard to be good because otherwise I might be trapped in London forever.

So I go over and I sit on the bed with my legs crossed and Dad grins like everything is just as it always was and he shows me a metal tin of round cards that his *physiotherapist* said was *the best game ever*. And I want to knock the cards to the ground and shout and tell him how much I miss the stretch of Stig's wings and the chirrup of her hungry cry and her orb eyes following me around the room but when I open my mouth he looks at me and he says

What feels best isn't always right, you know, October, October.

And there's such a look of sadness flickering on his face that I close my mouth and open the tin. And it's not the best game *ever* but it's fast and it's funny and it's clever and I keep remembering my crossness but then it's swallowed by the next matching picture and the scrabbling swipe to pick up the cards before he can and I'm nearly always faster but it's not that fair a race because his spine is a broken ladder at the moment.

He makes a quick-as-a-flash grab for a card and then he says *some things need to be wild, you know* and I stare down at my hands and the bright clean half-moon nails and the skin smoothed by the city. *October, October, sometimes it's a kindness to let something go even when you love it very much.* His voice is softer than rain-soaked soil and I push my fingers into the plasticky flesh of his mattress and I think of Stig with her wire-tangled view of the sky and I look at him but his eyes are watching a memory and I wonder if he's really thinking about Stig at all.

S he comes to collect me when the stars are starting to pinprick in the smoggy sky and the cold wraps around my bones and tingles my skin.

Sometimes it's a kindness to let something go even when you love it very much.

The words are wrapping around my bones too and they ache much more than the bite of the wind. I feel like something invisible is being cut and I am drifting and unconnected from Dad and from home and from my very own wild world.

The night smells like winter and earth and buses and the mingle of a thousand suppers caught on the wind. As we walk across the car park she stops

and points into the blackening gloom as a wisp of rust
flicks its tail and folds itself into the shadows. A fox.

Christmas in the woods is

fire fingers dancing in the grate

bonfire flames

sticky home-made toffee

white snow snapping under my boots

knitted stockings

a present wrapped in a hundred layers with something hidden in each one

climbing frost-dazzled branches

229

singing old songs to no music

toe-dipping the shivering pond

hot tea outside wrapped in blankets

perfect.

                    Christmas in London is

                        grey snow melting

                    a lonely tree dressed up

                its dying scent draining into the air

                        a new knitted stocking

                        that's not the same

                a heavy smell of fat and oil and grease

songs on the radio that I can't sing along to

inside inside inside

worry worry worry.

We go to visit Dad and I am nervous and my blood is sparking like flint in my veins. The roads are empty and there are no bright red bursts of buses and it feels like someone has shaken London upside down and tipped out all the people. I thought I might like it better this way but it feels like something is missing.

At the new hospital there are strings of shining bristles that look like glittering foxtails and another sad tree wrapped in strangling lights and all the nurses are wearing coloured hats and laughing and eating sweets wrapped up to look like jewels. The sharp clean scent is dusted with something spicy and something sweet and my tummy rumbles even though I've eaten two *mince pies* this morning once I found out they don't really have actual mince in them and then the Mars bar that was in the bottom of my stocking.

Dad is wearing a hat too and he's in his big chair and it makes him look like a strange king on a throne and he's got a glass of whisky and his eyes are bright and he's sitting up in a way that makes me think his bones and muscles aren't screaming so much today. He raises his glass to us and a nurse comes round with a drinks trolley *because it's Christmas* and the woman who is my mother gets a glass of dark wine and I choose a lemonade. The nurse puts cubes of ice in it and it's like drinking from the Antarctic. The lemonade fizzes on my tongue and goes up my nose and I sneeze and everyone laughs but it's delicious and sharp and sugary so I carry on sipping but slowly slowly.

I give Dad his ill-cat-that's-actually-a-reindeer card and it makes him laugh so much that I can see tears and I see a flash of something on her face. My heart is bursting because he likes it and I have to show him that he can't let me go but then he puts the card down and it slumps on to its side sadly and he doesn't even notice.

   We open presents together and there are more for
me than there have ever been before because I usually
only get one and it's usually something Dad has made
from the world around like my wooden treasure chest
or that he's secretly bought from the village like my
old yellow boots that I said I would throw away but
are hidden under my bed.

Today I get all for me

a notebook with
my name on the cover

                                        a pencil case
                        with trees painted on the sides
                              and pens in its belly

      bright green gloves
      she's knitted in secret
      snatched moments

a new trowel

a bucket with
my name looped
on the side in
gold letters

> and a big book about mudlarks
>> and their discoveries.

And everything is perfectly chosen and it feels like each thing has been made especially for me and some of it has and it's like if you could make me from a pile of things then it would be these things that built me. But I feel a bit like the pile of presents is pressing on my chest because there are so many and they're so very beautiful but I feel like they're pinning me to a new life and I don't know where to look or what to do with them all and I freeze. Dad shifts like his bones are starting to burst against his skin and he says *what do you say October, October, your mother went and got everything isn't it wonderful* but I can't get the words out and she puts her hand on my arm and says *bit much isn't it* and the air whizzes out of my chest and I nod and Dad says something that I don't hear because I say *thank you* and I look right at her and her eyes are bright and they're green like wild cherry leaves and they're green like mine.

When we get home I look at my presents and I open my notebook and I see in a swoop of thick blue ink that she has written

For all your stories

inside on the fresh new pages that are hungry for words.

I open my treasure box and I dig down and I find the Victorian key that could unlock anything or nothing or something and I put it on her pillow.

N ew Year's Eve in London is LOUD.

The woman who is my mother takes me to the same park that Yusuf and I scavenged in, except this time we look at the sky and not the ground. It's cold and the wind burns my cheeks and my hands are toasty warm in my green gloves. There are tangles of people everywhere and some of them are looped in bright glowing bands of light that break apart the darkness. She buys me one from a man with a whole tray of light strapped to his front and I stare at its luminous insides for the secret of its glow but I can't work it out and it's like a magic wand. She shows me how to wrap it around my wrist and when I *whoosh* my arm through the air I leave a trail of light like a firefly.

She tells me there will be lights in the sky too and that they will be *very very noisy* and says I should put my fingers in my ears, but I don't want to even when the booms and whistles and screeches start to echo in my brain. In the woods we have a bonfire for New Year and midnight smells like smoke and stars. Here at midnight the sky explodes into colours and it's terrifying and magical and awful and beautiful. Sparks and showers and stars and spangles of diamond dust and smoke are splashed against the stretched dark canvas of the night and it's wild and brave and brilliant and I love it I love it I love it.

On the first day of a whole new year we go and see Dad and he can stand upright when he's grabbing on to a bar and he takes some wobbly steps like a newborn deer but after three he slips backwards into a chair and there's a flush of sweat on his forehead and he swears for the first time I can ever remember.

This time last year we listened to the craw-craw-craw of a gang of stalk-legged crows while Dad felled three ash trees, and the magic from the fireworks dissolves in my mind and I am heartsick and worried that what we had has dissolved like those sparks in the sky.

I t is the first day back at school since the Christmas holidays cut a slice out of the year, and I didn't think I'd missed the rubbery smell of the school or the ear-exploding ring of the bell or the flat grey of the playground, but I see Yusuf hurling a furry yellow tennis ball at a wall and I feel a rush of something warm. I want to tell him about the fireworks and my new mudlarking presents, but he's crowded with people all jostling and whooping and telling him their news and so I put mine away for later.

Mr Bennett sits me and Yusuf down and he asks how we're getting on with our *assembly project* and we've done absolutely nothing at all. I know from

Yusuf that we can't tell him that, so I just nod while Yusuf says our *research* is going very well, which it isn't. My tummy is in knots and I feel sick. I know enough from the names on the board and the detentions and the letters to parents to know that not doing your schoolwork is a problem so huge that you could live inside it.

I try to talk to Yusuf about it at break but he is playing with the others and skipping rope and chanting numbers and I can't get my words to fit in the gaps he leaves. I chew on my raggedy fingernails and slump down a fence to watch and the rope twirls and leaps in front of me with nimble and quick feet sweeping over and under it and I think about Dad and three steps and it feels like he'll never get there. I just want to sit with Yusuf and talk about all the silly things like his brother, Ibi, microwaving a plastic bowl until it made a bright blue puddle that seeped out over everything and ruined the kitchen worktop, and I push my face into my hands and make the world go black. For a while I am suspended in the lonely darkness and the sounds around me fade until there's a tiny thump and the warmth of someone else. I peer through my fingers and see a pair of black shoes that look a lot like mine, except the laces on these have a daisy charm looped on to them. I turn my head to the left and Daisy smiles quietly at me and then looks away and down to the book in her lap. I sit next to Daisy until the bell breaks our silence and we walk back to lessons together.

Yusuf gives me a funny look when I sit next to Daisy in the classroom and not him, but within two seconds Tunde is beside him and they're using their pencils as swords and battling each other across the desk like knights in school jumpers. Daisy and I sit and look at the pages of her book together, and it's a beautiful story and I want to jump into the pages.

When the end-of-school bell screeches Yusuf ambles over to me with his schoolbag slung on one shoulder and he says *what's up with you, October* and I don't really know what to say to him. Just when I'm about to open my mouth Tunde and

Harry come up to Yusuf and throw a football at him and chant *let's play let's play* and Harry says *come on, mate* and my words scurry back inside my mouth. Yusuf shrugs and heaves his bag higher on his shoulder and starts towards the door and I suddenly shout

*You're supposed to be **my** friend and you're always leaving me*

and you won't even do our project together and you're letting me down again and again and again.

And my hands are balled into fists at my sides and the rage inside me feels hot and black.

Yusuf turns back in surprise and I can feel my cheeks light up like balls of fire. There is a flash of something on his face that I haven't seen there before and he says in a voice so quiet I almost don't catch his words *we don't have to be in a pair*

243

all the time you know and he walks out of the classroom towards Harry and Tunde and the waiting football.

I sit next to Daisy for the rest of the week and Yusuf swoops around his friends like a swallow.

The first mudlarking session after my first fight with my first friend is on Sunday. Yusuf and I stand a bit apart from each other on the stony foreshore and the wind bites us with ice-sharp teeth as it rushes across the flat river. I have my new bucket and my new trowel and my new gloves, but I put them in my pocket because I don't want to get them muddy, which isn't a thought I've ever had before. Yusuf has a new hat with a football badge on and the words *Manchester United* stitched under it, and I remember my maps and the finger-long stretch between London and Manchester and I think it's very far away.

Kate is telling us about a skeleton that was pulled from the Thames not very long ago and not very far away from right here and he was hundreds of years old and his bones were washed clean by the water and his long leather boots still nearly perfect on bound-together white bars and railings that were his feet. She overturns a rock and holds up a piece of something that turns out to be nothing and says *no one except mudlarks and fishermen wore long boots then so he was one of us* and I get a warm rush because she's saying I'm a mudlark and Yusuf is chanting *how did he die how did he die* and Kate shrugs and says *probably drowned maybe he fell asleep and the tide took him.*

I look at the river with a little shivery lick of fear because it is wild and it is dangerous and the tug of the moon can kill a person and keep them hidden and a secret for hundreds of years and I remember Tom from the Thames and his awful life and his tiny bones hidden away for years and never missed.

I keep looking for the answer to my secret ring. I flick and dig and scavenge with my hawk's eye but there is no glint of gold or flash of metal. The cold freezes my hands to red and then white and my fingers ache and my head howls. I can't find any stories today and especially not the one I most want to tell.

Kate calls us over and there's a flick of something in her voice and even Tilly looks interested. But when we've picked our way over the rocks and pebbles I can't see anything that's exciting at all. Kate is holding a lump of rock and grinning so widely I can count her teeth. Yusuf looks at Tilly and Tilly looks at me and I look at Kate and she rolls her eyes and tells us we *have a lot to learn*. She pours water from her drink bottle over the lump and I wait for the water to reveal a diamond or a gemstone or a piece of gold from a pirate's treasure chest. Yusuf is hopping from one foot to the other because he's certain he was just about to find gold coins in his patch.

Then there's a
shimmer and a
shine.

A flash of sunlight
made metal.

The slice of a circle.

My heart tumbles and turns.

A glimmer of gold.

It has to be.

I wish it could have been me who found it and I wish I had been searching close to the nibbling edge of the river where Kate had been standing. But it doesn't matter as long as I have my ring and I'll have the other half of the secret and two things that fit together perfectly and a story that is whole and spins like a sphere.

248

My heart is beating cherry red in my chest and my breath is sitting unused in my lungs.

Kate washes away more of the grime and the river's spit and Yusuf sucks in his own breath with a *whoosh*.

Her thumb scrapes at grooves and ridges and bumps.

It's not my ring.

A gold coin lies flat in her palm. A full circle with metal stretched edge to edge. I clench my fists until the arced imprints of my nails have bitten into my flesh while Yusuf and Tilly rush forward to look properly. Yusuf is chattering away about pirates and treasure and Tilly is running her fingers around the edges of the coin as it sits in Kate's hand. I turn so that they won't see the start of the tears that are beading at the corners of my eyes and I stamp back to my bucket.

October?

Kate's hand drops on to my shoulder and I jump. She steps back a little and then holds out her other hand, the coin lying flat and useless in the dip of her palm.

Do you want to see?

The metal winks at me in the pale sunlight and it's like it's laughing at me and my stupid ideas. I take the coin and hold it up to the iron sky rippled with clouds and I feel it heavy between my fingers and I

hurl it back into the water where it sinks beneath
the mystery of the river
and is gone.

Kate isn't exactly angry. She doesn't shout or say bad words or clench her fists or pace up and down. She doesn't do anything at all except tell Tilly and Yusuf to keep searching *but don't you dare dig more than three and a half inches or I'll have your guts for garters* and then she asks me to follow her as she walks slowly along the edge of the river where the coin is hidden under steely water. She doesn't say anything and her eyes are down and roaming across the stones and mine do the same but I don't see anything except the flash of my own wellies.

The silence grows and it roars and gapes. I want to

plug it with words but just like always I can't find the right ones and they melt in my mouth before I can shape them and they taste bitter. I spit them away and Kate looks up at me and says *that's gross* and I swallow and whisper *sorry*. She nods and says *that was a really great find, why'd you do it* and I twist my cold fingers and I tell her *because it wasn't what I thought it was*.

Kate looks surprised and hurt and I took something away from her just like they took Stig away from me and I know what that feels like and suddenly all the words I've been wanting to say tumble out in jumbles and knots and tangles and I tell her about Dad falling and Dad's starbust spine and how it's all my fault and about the woods and pond jumps and hospitals and Stig and wild skies and wire cages and the woman who is my mother and London and school and the assembly and the ring and secrets and stories and how I can't tell them right any more and about my fight with Yusuf. I tell her the other ring is the perfect end to the perfect story and how I can't find the words to tell it and without finding the ring I will never be able to get Dad to forgive me and he loves me but he's going to let me go.

She must be smoothing everything I say into sense in her head because she nods and says *this is what I love about mudlarking, you know* and I don't know but she carries on.

It shows us a little moment from someone's life, a secret or a treasure or a something as simple as the boots they wore every day. But it just shows us that one thing. Just those little moments. Do you know what flotsam and jetsam are?

I shake my head no but I like the lightness of the words.

Stuff lost to the water, that was never meant to be there. Thrown overboard or spilled in a shipwreck. Discarded objects. Moments. The world is jumbled up and things don't always end up where they were supposed to be. Those things might be able to tell us a little something about something, but they don't tell us the full story of how someone felt or what someone thought or what they wanted or who they really were.

And everything is so much bigger than that, isn't it? So we fill in the rest. We create tales and fill in the blanks and sketch out the stories. We put things in what we think are the right places. That's what you've done with what your dad said, you know. But it's not real. You don't need a ring to fix things, October. Your lives aren't just made up of flotsam and jetsam, of discarded moments, of something spun in your mind. You know who your dad is. He knows who you are. You know every moment of your lives together. You know each other's stories and you both know he doesn't need a story to love you so very much in this very real world of ours, and he will never ever let you go or give you up.

She scans the ground for another minute and picks up a piece of rock that's an ancient arrowhead and holds it up. Not everything has a perfect place. And not every story has a perfect end. But that bit is up to you, isn't it?

I feel the world around me is breaking open just a little bit. I have to burst through and I have to do something and I have to be brave and I have to be wild.

I feel something inside me lighten and lift for the first time in forever. I don't need to find the ring to tie me to Dad. I can do that myself.

Kate claps her hand on to my back and says *I might be able to help with Mr Dinosaur Boots over there though, all right?*

She calls Yusuf over and he looks at the ground and digs his dinosaur-covered toe into the mud. Kate asks him what's happened and his cheeks go red and he says he shouted and he's sorry and he should have worked on the project, and I feel a bloom of guilt because I shouted first and it's not fair that I want to be Yusuf's only friend and I should have done some work too. I say it all and Yusuf sticks his damp and muddy hand out and I shake it exactly like before like a fox with a rabbit and he yelps with laughter.

Kate looks pleased and she pretends to cuff us both round the ear for being silly and then she straightens up and says *Now, what's this about a school assembly?*

And when I get home I write down the words she used in my new notebook and I read them over and over again and there's a plan.

That afternoon we drive to the owl rescue, and this time will be the last time.

Stig is strong.

Stig is wild.

Stig is being released.

The sky is open for her.

It is dusk and the light is melting darkly into stars. Jeff has put Stig in a special wooden box inside a new wire cage in the middle of a field near the rescue centre. I can't see her but I can hear her screeches and her squawks. They sound different and louder but I still know it's her and my heart tugs. Jeff has put on a pair of gloves that remind me of the single black falconer's glove that is still under my pillow in London, all empty and unused and alone and useless. The tug turns into a bruise.

We have to hide when we let her out, OK says Jeff and he points at a wooden wall with slits cut in it so we can see through. The woman who is my mother nods and whispers *this is wonderful for her, October* and I almost nod back because this might not be my perfect ending but it's Stig's.

Jeff goes into the big cage and opens a door in the wall and then opens the door of Stig's box. He slips back out of the big cage and we duck behind the wooden wall to watch. I can hear my own breathing filling the space around us and my heart catches and falls and spins.

Stig pokes her beak out first. Then slowly the rest

of her emerges. She is beautiful. Her flight feathers have filled in and her chest has puffed out. Her eyes are paintbrush flicks in a heart face and her fluff has smoothed itself into white china. She looks strong and delicate all at once and she hops up to the platform by the opening on to the world. She opens her beak and tests the air with her voice. She's calling for me. I want to run to her and close the cage and sit on the ground with her on my lap and sing her stupid songs and throw her mice and stroke her feathers and never ever let her go but

she stretches her wings so wide

the tips brush against the edges of the wire

she hops just a little

then more

and she flaps

and there's a burst of air and feathers and bright white and gold

and she's swooping into the dusk

free.

She swerves in the open sky and turns and dives and loops and it's better than fireworks and snow and scavenging and bonfires and pond jumps and tree climbs. She is truly wild.

There is a gold glimmer. A flash. Just a moment but I see it before she disappears into the night and from me.

I can't cry, I won't cry, so I ask about the flash of gold and Jeff says *that's her ring. We ring all our birds so we can check on their progress. It's got a special number in it so we know just who she is.* He stops for a moment and doesn't say anything even though his mouth is open and then he looks a bit embarrassed and he scratches his head and his cheeks glow red. *I'm not meant to do this really but I put her name in too. So she'll always be a name as well as a number. Stig 2450. That's her forever. Without you she wouldn't be much at all eh, and you gave her that name. So a bit of you is with her always eh.* Then he shuffles off quickly to pick up the box and the cage and I can hear the woman who is my mother crying.

It was the right thing I whisper and she squeezes my green-gloved hand tight.

Yusuf keeps rearranging the table and it's making me itch inside. He puts the clay pipes at the front and then he puts them at the back and then he moves the little heap of blackened coins to the middle and he makes them into a Y just like with the bottle caps but then that doesn't look right either and he's muttering to himself and he's nervous. I'm nervous too but I don't know what to do with the sparking feeling so I sit on my hands to stop them tingling and think about not being sick instead.

Today we have to show the whole of Years Five and Six our special assembly. An assembly we're meant to have been working on for months. An assembly that didn't exist until four days ago.

I can't climb a tree and escape.

I can't keep my mouth closed and put my fingers in my ears and imagine myself into a whole new world far away.

This is the wildest I think I've ever had to be.

The doors of the big hall open and Kate walks in and some of the air that's been caught inside my chest hisses out and I think I might not have to be sick in the bin just yet.

The plan.

Kate hoists two huge bags full of treasures on to the table and she squeezes my shoulder and grins like she does this every single day and says *all right, trouble* to Yusuf and he sticks his tongue out but in a nice way. She starts to take out her finds and they're the best things ever. Shoes and teeth and whole vases and animal skulls and a real person's skull and a hat that's older than the building we're in right now and coins worth more than a car but *not like a Porsche or anything* according to Yusuf and all the little fragments that build up whole lives.

Kate is folding black bin bags and she disappears for a few minutes and comes back with sacks of sand from a gardening centre. Yusuf and I spread it out across the stage. Kate keeps coming back with more and more sand until there is a foreshore on the stage and the Thames has been transported into our school and I think I can even smell the scent of tides and seagulls and mud. We don't have that many rocks because Kate couldn't fit all of the sand in the car and we couldn't take too many stones from the foreshore anyway but it looks *brilliant* breathes Yusuf.

And we hide some of our treasures as secrets in the sand.

When Years Five and Six come stamping into the hall and the noise bubbles up to the roof I feel ready.

Yusuf and I have to do a little bit of a speech about mudlarking. He does his bit perfectly and his face is bright and his words are too, even though we only thought of them last night over beans on toast at the kitchen table. The faces turned up towards him are rapt and hungry for more.

And then Yusuf steps to the side with a hoppity bow that makes the audience laugh, and I'm on my own.

I think my words might get stuck again but I fling them out into the crowd and they fly just like I hoped they would and the feeling is like pond jumping and fireworks and an owl flying free.

I tell them about the children who mudlarked all those years ago and about Tom from the Thames and the long-booted skeleton and the gold coin and finally I tell them about my super-secret ring with its half a message and

I tell them that we'll never know where the other ring is.

That not every story has just one perfect ending.

That stories can change along the way.

And then Yusuf and I read them the stories we

made up in our last few library sessions. When I stopped looking the stories found me. We magic up a world that might exist and it might not and our imaginations are like a spell and the finds table is a portal to a world that we can build and twist and turn and spin into anything we want.

Then Years Five and Six get to hunt for their own stories and there are shouts and yelps and whoops and so much excitement that it fills me from my toes to the top of my head. Harry finds a coin and Maryam uses one of the trowels to dig up a ferry token and Lily holds a scrap of hand-painted pottery swirled with flowers just like her name. Mr Bennett finds a clay pipe and the knees of his smart trousers are scuffed with sand but he's delighted and he tells Zara that it belonged to a distinguished gentleman who had no children and six dogs that he tucked into bed at night.

Daisy comes towards me and she's holding a piece of river glass. It is brushed dull by the sand but it glows green in her outstretched palm. She reaches me and smiles and says *can you tell me its story,* *October? I'm not good at thinking of them like you are.* And I'm not smooth and fluid around my edges like Yusuf and I stumble on my words and I am stiff in my shoulders but together we start to work out the world that the treasure came from.

By the end of the assembly Kate has a long list of children signed up to come along to the Tide and Thames club.

And I'm so happy.

In class we spend the whole afternoon writing the stories of our finds. We have brand-new exercise books specially for it but I use my Christmas note-book and I write down the story of the ring. It can be any secret I want and the possibilities dance from my pen until I find what I want.

The other half of the ring belongs to an owl flying free.

Let neither friend nor foe this secret know
In the wild world flies Stig 2450.

And it's my best story yet and it's pieces of woods and water and Dad and me and Yusuf and Kate and the whole wild world that tumbles around me. It is my story and it is our story and it isn't perfect and it isn't finished but it is whole.

The assembly we did was so popular that Ms Everett asks us to leave the hall like it is so all the other classes can have a go at mudlarking and she asks us if we'll give our little speeches again and she sends out an email which Yusuf reminds me is like a letter but through time and space.

The email invites parents.

I don't say anything about it just in case she hasn't seen it but she gives me the biggest smile when she picks me up and she says she can't wait to come to school and see all my hard work and I mutter something that doesn't even make sense in my own head and go upstairs to read a book.

There are a lot more people here this time. Children and parents and siblings and teachers all in knots and bundles and lines. We've made the foreshore even bigger with help from Mr Bennett and from Kate's endless supply of sandbags. They stayed late to make sure it was just right for us today. It's not on the stage any more and it's the whole floor of the hall and I don't really want to think about how we're going to clear up all that sand because it might take years.

It's crowded and loud and hot and bright but I can swallow all of that down. I know those sounds and sights and smells now and it's OK. It's not the best thing but it's OK.

Yusuf and I stand on a little stage made of just two boxes. I'm nervous again but Mr Bennett gave us tips on how to keep calm like *imagining everyone in their pants* which sounds like the opposite of something to calm you down and *staring at a fixed point in the distance* and *speaking in the loudest clearest voice that you own*. I keep staring at the clock at the back of the hall and not at all the faces so I don't fall off my box with my wobbly legs and so I don't look for her face. We do a bit of our talk and then some of our class read their stories aloud and everyone claps and then we carry on and I tell them about the ring again.

And I start to read my story about my owl and being wild and being free and the biggest secret of all is knowing what that means for you and about loving things and letting them go and endings that aren't perfect. And I look up into the faces bobbing like a sea of wild flowers. And I see them.

She's there.

And so is he.

Dad.

And he's standing upright and tall and he's wearing clothes that aren't from a hospital and he's there he's there he's there and he's smiling and he looks right at me and his face is alight with something new and familiar all at once and I haven't seen him look like that since the fall and I feel a rush of something uncomplicated and beautiful and perfect flash between us.

And my heart is soaring and breaking and bird-beating but I read my story in the *loudest clearest voice* that I own just like Mr Bennett said I should.

And when I'm finished I get off my box and I run across our foreshore and I am swept into a circle of arms.

And it feels just like home.

Dad stays in the London house with us because he can't go back to the woods just yet. There's too much chopping and hauling and lifting and digging and moving to keep it warm and to keep us fed, and even though Bill has been keeping our growing tunnel alive there's still a lot to do. Dad sleeps in the living room so he doesn't have to climb the stairs and I'm bursting with excitement because I've got so much for him to see and we have so much to catch up on. He's still sleepy and stiff and just going to the park makes him sleep for four hours when we get back and it seems like it'll be forever before he can spring about like a boxing hare like before but he says it won't be long at all.

We take things slowly. At first I show him things near the house like the park and the garden shed and the woman who is my mother shows us how to melt and shape metal into something new but it's much harder than it looks and we're rubbish. I like burning the metal until it glows and the copper goes the best dark cherry red. I give her handfuls of river glass for her overflowing jars and drawers of found things and she says *thank you* with surprised eyebrows and she promises to make it into something beautiful.

I want to show Dad the Thames and the mudlarking museum and the red buses but he's too tired and his face is always grey. It's like the city is seeping into his bones and blooming into his skin and I want to get him away from here because it'll never make him better. He needs the trees and the call of the birds and the wide open air stretching his lungs.

One evening I whisper to him the thoughts I've been afraid to turn into words and I ask him if he wants to leave me here. He cups my face in his hands that are smooth from months of being still and inside and he looks right into my leaf-green eyes and he asks me if I want to stay.

And there's a sudden beat of silence that's full of a million unsaid things and I realise he's afraid.

He says in a rush *I never knew if this was the right thing, if the woods were the right place, if the way I lived was fair. But you didn't want to go and I couldn't let you go but if you're happier here then I understand, October, October, I understand.*

And his voice trembles and fades into dust.

And I fold myself into his arms and I tell him I want to go home.

here are crocuses peeping through the ground when we go back to the woods.

Before we go I say goodbye to Year Six and Mr Bennett. We have a little party and he brings a cake with a tiny tree made of sugar paste sitting on the top and I get to keep it. *Eat it eat it* chant Yusuf and Harry but I don't because it's perfect in miniature and I slip it in my pocket for my treasure chest and I join in the mad dancing to songs on YouTube which is where you find every video of every single thing in the world.

I say goodbye to Yusuf after school in the park but it's not really goodbye because Dad will bring me to Tide and Thames every single Sunday and when it's not on because of the holidays Yusuf and I and all the millions of new members will hunt in the park instead but I still have to bite the inside of my cheek so I don't cry. He gives me a Mars bar and I give him a story. It's about a wild boy in the wild city jungle and how he finds a whole new world beneath his feet in the twists and tunnels of London.

I let myself into the terraced sandwiched house with the red door which isn't mine any more and that feels strange. I walk through the hallway and no one calls out to me and that feels strange too.

Upstairs in the stark white room that was my bedroom everything has changed.

The walls aren't white any more. The walls are a forest all around.

She has made my room into the woods.

Smooth black trunks and lime-green leaves stuck on the walls and branches creeping around corners and the outline of a squirrel blending into bark and a

277

bird swooping through the canopy and up to a starry ceiling. The old empty bookshelves are gone and instead the branches of the painted trees are somehow loaded with a brilliant xylophone of rainbow spines. Book trees. Just for me.

It's for when you come back she whispers and then her next words are feather light

                                        if you want to.

And I stand in my wild room in my wild city and I put my arms around my wild mother and I tell her *I do I do I do* and then I say

Thank you

              Mum

and the name soars.

I t is October and this is my month. We've jumped in the pond and it was warmer this year but it still felt head-spilling and wild and we still roared and yelped and crashed through the water in an explosion of crystal sparks and we splashed in the deep green and warmed up our bones with blankets and tea and flames.

It is October and today I am twelve and we are planting an oak.

But it's not just us in the woods today.

Cars are going to rumble down the track.

Feet are going to crunch the burnt-orange ground.

People are coming to the woods. My woods. For

the very first time. Yusuf and his family and Daisy and her mum and Kate and Mr Bennett and it's too many to think about.

It feels like our tiny universe has been sliced open for the first time and the outside is starting to spill in. I'm not going to hide in a tree, even though my palms are damp and my heart is trembling.

Dad and I have strung streamers from all my favourite trees and they ripple their colours into the air and I think they look beautiful but what if Yusuf laughs and thinks they're for babies and what if he thinks the woods are strange and what if he doesn't like the pond or our ramshackle little house or the smell of the leaves or the horizon of trees? What if he can't see the beauty in the small things?

I've never had to worry about people not thinking my woods are beautiful before and I want to hide them away. They're a little bit more ragged than usual because Dad is still slowly slowly getting faster and stronger. He got Bill's son to come and help him this summer and he says he might do that a bit more even when he's completely better.

I want to cancel the whole thing and hide under my quilt.

Yusuf and his family are the first to arrive and he flings a present at me and then starts trying to climb the first tree he sees and immediately falls off. Ibi rolls his eyes and he and his girlfriend, Yasmin, hug me and say *happy birthday* and they're the third and fourth people ever to say that to me.

Yusuf runs from tree to tree and when he sees my den he screeches like a fox. Dad and I fixed it up over the summer after the winter had twisted it and we added a tiny camping stove and I painted the walls with stories like cave people used to do and some of my finds are hanging on loops of string from the sloping ceiling. My Mum-made navy starry O blanket has been rescued from the bottom of my wardrobe and it's draped over an old wicker chair. Yusuf is bouncing from corner to corner and he's saying *this is so cool how did you do this* and *I want one* and *do you think I could fit one on a balcony* and he looks up to the treasure-spangled ceiling and stops to touch each thing gently with the tips of his fingers and my heart is slowing down a little bit.

Kate and her boyfriend are here and he's Mr Bennett or *call-me-David-but-only-on-the-weekends* and it's strange to think of him as anyone's boyfriend because he's a teacher and Yusuf says it's *gross* but he comes on our mudlarking Sundays sometimes and he's got eagle eyes and he found a tiny real gold charm on his first trip. It's in a museum now. Yusuf called it *beginner's luck* but he follows Mr Bennett around a lot on the foreshore now.

Daisy and her mum rattle down the track in a bright green car that looks like a bug and she gets out wearing wellies that look brand new. She seems tiny surrounded by all the reaching trees and there's a flicker on her face and it's like she's frozen by wonder and she whispers in a little voice that lifts on the breeze

It's so beautiful

And she stretches her arms wide and lifts her face to the leafy canopy and she beams.

We have a scavenger hunt that Mum set up yesterday when she arrived. Usually I visit her on the weekends because I go to school in the village during the week now, and when I'm at our house in London I help her make delicate loops of silver necklaces. I stay in my forest room in the middle of the muddle of the city, so it's funny and strange and brilliant to have her in my real woods in my different world. She is alive in London in the same way Stig is alive in the wild and Dad is alive in the woods.

The scavenger hunt is cheating a bit because she's planted all the treasure and we have to follow clues to find more clues to find more clues to get the prize. It takes a long time because the clues are so clever and cunning that we have to squeeze our brains hard to solve them and when the meaning clicks into place we hare off like a pack of wild wolves to find the next one. When we've solved them all we find a treasure chest nestled in the hollow of a tree bursting with jewel-bright sweets and little wooden bird-call whistles that Dad makes at the fireside every evening. I choose an owl call and I hoot into the sky and I hope one day I see her.

After the scavenger hunt we eat baked potatoes straight from the fire and Yusuf says they're the best thing he's ever eaten. We play games and sing songs and the woods are still our tiny pocket of wildness, but I don't think we have to be wild alone any more.

When the party is over and the cars have grumbled back up the track we sit by the fire as the night wraps around us and I drink a spit of whisky and we tell stories and Mum gives me something magical. Something she's made just for me.

Happy birthday, October, October.

A little black box which is soft like a rabbit's belly fur. I snap it open and sparkling inside is a gold ring with chips of coloured glass set in the top like a sphere of glowing light. *River glass and wood glass* she whispers. My magic stones slipped under Dad's pillow all those months ago. *And just a tiny slice of moonstone* and she taps her own ring that glints in the firelight. My ring is just the right size for my bony finger. I trace the writing curled on the inside.

Stig 2450

Sometimes at night I hear the soft call of an owl and sometimes I think I see the blink of a gold ring against the inky sky and I hope that she's in the wild wide space above my head and I know we are linked forever.

Stig is free and I am free. Being wild and free is different for every person and every thing and it can be folded into the woods or whirling through the city streets. I know not everything has a perfect ending and I know that some things have a perfect place and that some things don't and that all this can change anyway. I am wild in the woods and wild in the city and I have a foot stamped in each world and it's wonderful. The lines of my life scribble over the edges of these magical places and there's brilliance in both.

I can be a pair and I can be alone and I complete myself and many other people complete me too. There is still so much to see and do and Yusuf and I are going to travel the world and find wildness wherever we go.

There are stories everywhere and I want to tell them all.

And all the world is wild and waiting for me.

Acknowledgements

Firstly I have to thank the incredible Lucy Mackay-Sim. I am so lucky to have such a skilful, clever and nuanced editor. Some writers dread their edits – I never have, because your thoughts and ideas are always exactly what is needed and so perfectly pitched. Your editing skills make me a better writer, and also you always choose excellent restaurants.

Thank you to the whole Bloomsbury team – Beatrice Cross, Jade Westwood, Fliss Stevens, Stephanie Amster, Anna Swan and Sarah Taylor-Fergusson. I am so grateful for all your hard work and for just how lovely you all are.

Angela Harding, for your wonderful depictions of a growing Stig (trust me, it's not easy to make a baby barn owl look good, they're disgusting) and the most beautiful front cover I could ever have imagined. You brought October's world to life.

289

Catherine Clarke, my amazing agent, for being so clever and sharp and sure – thank you. And to everyone at Felicity Bryan Associates, especially Robin Ganderton for his A+ correspondence game.

Leah Carden, for juggling being an actual important human with a grown-up job and also finding the time to help me with plots and medical questions – thank you. Your help is invaluable and I am so grateful. Miranda Prag, queen of the waterways, thank you for confidence, humour and a long friendship based on a shared love of retired Suffolk farmworkers. Gaby Aberbach, for your other-worldly kindness, challah French toast and meanders through meadows. To Tony Ozgu, the world's best barman – thank you for wonderful evenings away from writing. And stop giving away so many free drinks, it's a terrible business model.

My writing gang, for writing support, but mostly for Ghibli marathons, cocktails and aggressive quizzing: Aisha Bushby, Joseph Elliott, Holly Jackson, Sarah Ann Juckes, Struan Murray and Yasmin Rahman.

My parents, Malcolm Balen and Karen Meager, for unwavering support in every single way, and for showing me stories everywhere. I am finding it difficult to say exactly how much you have done for me, and continue to do for me. But I do know how lucky I am to have such parents. To my brother, Mischa, who is generous and kind: thank you, and put your cat on a diet.

Bob Simpson, who lives off-grid in his own actual forest, just like October: thank you for The Wilderness and thank you for taking the time to teach me about trees. And for bucket owl, where this whole thing started.

Patrick Simpson, who would rather be in the forest but lives a London life with me. I don't tell you enough how proud I am of everything you do, and how none of this would be possible without you being the brilliant man that you are. You are the very best of people, and I am so profoundly lucky. Thank you.

Have you read

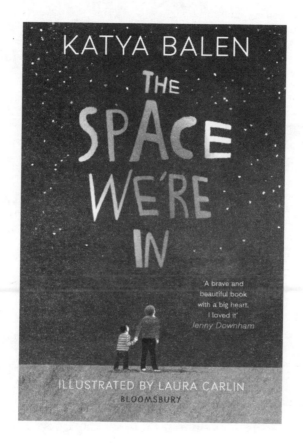

KATYA BALEN

THE
SPACE
WE'RE
IN

'A brave and
beautiful book
with a big heart.
I loved it'
Jenny Downham

ILLUSTRATED BY LAURA CARLIN

BLOOMSBURY

AVAILABLE NOW

Turn the page for a sneak peek ...

13 5 12 20 4 15 23 14

I am ten and Max is five.
There are twenty-six days until Max
starts school and we're going to buy
new shoes for the new school. We've
looked at his hard plastic book with its
little Velcro-y laminated pictures that
show him what's happening now and
next. It has a blue silky smooth strap so he
can wear it round his neck when we're not at
home and he needs to know what's going to
happen. He doesn't like the weight and the
click-clack of the plastic pages though so Mum
carries it for him instead. Mum showed him the
pictures of shoes and the shop and we whirled

around the world on Google Street View trying to find the shop to show him so he's prepared but it's not there so she's worried worried worried. I went to Egypt on Google Street View and I showed Max but he was jumping up and down so he didn't get to look at the pyramids. Now we are in the car. *New shoes new school* Mum says to Max. Max doesn't say anything because he never says anything and he doesn't stop humming even though I ask him to stop humming.

I'm not going to a new school but I'm getting new shoes. I think that might be confusing Max, so I tell him that I'm not going to a new school. *You are* I say. *You're going to a new school*. Max keeps humming. I tell him to shut up and Mum doesn't say *don't tell your brother to shut up, Frank* because she's worried about the new shoes new school.

We get to the shoe shop and Mum parks the car too close to a wall so I have to wait in my seat while she gets Max out. She puts his reins on and I say *giddy-up* but she doesn't laugh. Max flaps his hands and Mum shows him his special book and I say *new shoes!* but Max doesn't like that. Mum tells him words using her hands, she says *new* and she says *first shoes, then biscuit* but Max isn't looking so he can't listen.

We go into the shop and Max is still humming so people look at him. I used to tell people he was talking but I don't say that any more. The shop is big, too big for Max. I don't see anyone I know and that makes me happy but it's not the sort of happy that makes me smile. I go and look at cool shoes with high tops and long laces and I hold them up and Mum doesn't say no because she's telling the shoe lady that she can't touch Max's feet but that Mum thinks they're a size two. The lady says she'd like to measure Max because they don't like to sell shoes that don't fit and wouldn't it be easier not to have to bring them back? Mum smiles but she's not smiling really, and says that she just wants the same shoes Max is wearing but bigger and if we have to come back we will just come back.

Max is humming louder and louder and his hands are flapping down by his sides and not up in the air so

I think we might have to go. Mum talks to Max with her hands and gives him a ball to squish with his hands because that might stop them flapping. I am still looking at trainers with ticks and not school shoes because I won't get them today because Max doesn't like this.

The lady isn't happy and she says to Max to come here so she can have *a little look-see* at his feet. I want to tell her to shut up but I don't want to say anything at all so I just look at all the tick trainers with high tops and I choose ones with blue laces. I pick them up and check the size and it's perfect for me. The shoe-shop lady says *lots of little boys don't like having their feet measured* and she's *sure he'll be fine*, and that *he's a brave boy and there are stickers for brave boys* and *does he like football* because she has football stickers and *does he play football or support a football team or perhaps he likes Match Attax cards because little boys like those a lot, don't they?* And then it's too many words and Max is having his meltdown.

I don't know why they call it that, because when

something like ice melts it pours itself into a puddle and it isn't hard any more. When Max melts he's the hardest thing in the world and you think he's going to explode his bones from his body. He bites and bites and bites at his fists and his humming is a scream from his chest and nose and mouth. He is fury and he's lost himself and everyone and everything and everywhere.

All the people in the shop are looking at the furious biting boy even though they're grown-ups and it's rude to stare and the shop lady doesn't say anything any more. I don't stare. Mum is using her hands again to say *finished finished finished* and she says it with her mouth too. She picks Max up because he is stiff and small and not a puddle but he kicks and lashes and twists himself *hisssss* like a snake. His fingers are in his ears because he doesn't like the sound he's making and then the two of them push out through the door and Mum holds his reins as he gallops.

I put back the tick trainers with blue laces.

Finished finished f i n i s h e d.